The Eunuch Warrior

Zhang Li

The Eunuch Warrior

A novel set in fifteenth century China. It charts the events leading up to, and the lives of, Hoong and Yiling, who meet and fall in love but are separated by war.

Hoong is captured and emasculated, but emerges from the depths of despair convinced that his life's task is to protect his country from its enemies. The courageous, talented youth is the eunuch warrior, training soldiers and leading teams to extend and reinforce the Great Wall, rising to outstanding general, securing China's northwestern border in the Gobi Desert.

Yiling becomes the young wife of an older aristocrat, not the life that she expected or wanted, but accepts. She is protected, loved and provided for, yet cannot escape an inner emptiness. Intelligent, sensitive and perceptive, she devotes herself to the less fortunate. In a world where women are often disregarded, she sees many abandoned wives. Her first charity is a home for such women. Yiling also has a deep-held belief that all female children are born free and should not be victim to the custom of foot binding. She does what she can to rescue young females from this painful, sometimes deadly fate.

Hoong and Yiling are the young lovers who dared to dream and hope. They reached for happiness together, instead finding separation, sorrow and pain, even while making meaningful contributions to their society. But life also brings the unexpected. There is reunion. In middle age they find the bliss they dreamt of in their youth, achieving contentment and peace. Love prevails.

Love is timeless, so too sorrow and joy. Does it matter that the story is set in the fifteenth century? It could be the first century BC or the 21st century AD!

THE EUNUCH WARRIOR

Contents

Note to the reader

This story is a work of fiction. While many of the events and characters existed, the lives of Hoong and Yiling spring from the imagination of the author, as do the city of Jian'an and the state of Hu.

All the illustrations herein were specifically created for this novel using the online NightCafe Creator AI tool.

2

Author's Message

To me, The Eunuch Warrior is more than a fairy tale. There are many facts interwoven with my imaginary city of Jian'an. I want those who know little of China to learn something of its history and culture, for it is worth knowing. The Eunuch Warrior is not just a tale of handsome heroes and beautiful heroines, of power and splendour, but of human emotions, which are universal and timeless! The period I chose for this novel is the early fifteenth century in Ming dynasty China.

Fate plays tricks on us, just as it does in the present day. There are accidents, incidents and tragedies.

It was a chance accident that led to Hoong's castration and denied him the life of an ordinary person. He was too old for the procedure. There is much cruelty in this world of ours, but it is the only world we know. We are also reluctant to leave it! At the same time there is so much beauty surrounding us. Best of all, there is so much love in this imperfect world. The downtrodden can make something of themselves. We have challenges and we have rewards. The characters in my novel are able to rise and achieve.

If we can understand life a little better and accept what we cannot change, then perhaps, just perhaps, we will be able to lead a more meaningful life!

Zhang Li

3

A Tale of Two Homelands

The story of China is not merely a history of the Han people. In reality, it is a story of the tribal nomads who lived to the north of China and their interactions with the Chinese. These outer "barbarians" lived a nomadic life in contrast to the sedentary Chinese, who practised agriculture and lived a settled life, mostly in fertile Inner China. With the passage of time, the arts flourished in the cities south of the grasslands. Chinese architecture was springing up everywhere. Not only did the grand mansions of the wealthy dot the landscape, but the ornate palaces of the rulers, who lived in luxury, became bigger and more numerous. The wealthy had time for learning, calligraphy, painting, for wine, women and song.

Genghis Khan was known to despise the soft life of the Chinese, while Emperor Jia Jing of the early Ming dynasty had nothing but contempt for the barbarians!

The domain of the so-called wild tribes stretched all the way across northern China. In the northeast were the Xiong Nu, ancestors of the Mongols, so too the Jurchens, who produced the Manchurians. There were the Gokturks in the centre, and moving westwards, the Kitans, Uyghurs and Tibetans.

The tribes not only fought and raided the Chinese towns across the border, they fought each other and formed temporary alliances when it was beneficial. The Han dynasty historian Sima Qian (145 - 86 BC) wrote of them as tribes who moved their herds from place

3

to place, that they grew no food and preyed on others weaker than them. Sima Qian went on to say that these tribes had no writing, no learning, no rules to govern the young, that "they know nothing of righteousness." Yet the Mongols and the Manchurians conquered and respectively ruled China as the Yuan dynasty from 1279 to 1368 and the Ching dynasty from 1644 to 1912.

Thus, the history of China is so much a part of these tribes.

A great deal of beauty surrounded the lives of these nomads. There was the rugged beauty of the snow-covered mountains in winter, placid lakes and the lush grasslands in summer. A harsh magnificent landscape where sucking in the cold air could hurt the ill and sickly babies could not survive the winter. But those who lived grew tall, strong and tough. These became the expert horsemen, the warriors who could kill while riding, for they were outstanding archers and swordsmen too. On their homeland, the Steppes, these warriors roamed wild and free.

While Chinese youth practised calligraphy and learnt the classics, the tribal youth practised archery and hunting. The Chinese boys flew kites and learnt about wind speeds, while the tribal boys practised falconry and enjoyed the wind out in the open. According to some sources, falconry had its origins in Mongolia, beginning somewhere between 6,000 to 4,000 BC. Wrestling was also recorded as a sport among the Mongolians, youths pitting their strength against each other and embracing the camaraderie.

The two homelands were so different, yet each had its own beauty and charm. While nature seemed to spawn the physically fit, nurture was to produce the famous Chinese paintings and poetry passed down the years.

The Great Wall of China was built for the security of the Chinese citizens due to fear of these tribes. The three great building periods occurred when China had strong empires: firstly during the time of Qin Shi Huang Ti, famed for the Terracotta Army, secondly during the Han dynasty, and thirdly during the Ming dynasty. Small sections of the Wall were built by various rulers at other times. However, during the golden period of the Tang dynasty (618 – 907 AD), a time when China was strong and prosperous and the barbarian tribes rather subdued, there was not much wall building. The ancient overland trade routes, now known as the Silk Road, flourished during this time.

Needless to say, the building of the Great Wall, even stretches of it, was a massive project that required vast resources and manpower. It was not merely the forced labour of locals, peasants and farmers, but soldiers to oversee them and the need to feed them. According to one estimate, half million men died building the Wall. There were stories told of many a young builder interred in the Wall and the young wives who came in search of them.

The Great Wall spanned grasslands, mountains and deserts, extending over terrain where the tribes roamed. Watchtowers were often built at the highest points, requiring men of intelligence to source and transport the necessary supplies. The ingenuity of the Chinese engineers and planners is seldom remembered or given due praise. During the Ming dynasty, planners introduced the double walls and secret tunnels. The tunnels allowed the Ming soldiers to surprise and massacre encamped tribal warriors before they could attack.

The Ming military built gates at strategic points. Indeed, it was through the gates at a vital pass, the Shan Hai Guan, that the Manchurian armies came. Shan Hai Guan was the eastern-most stronghold along the Ming Great Wall. It was betrayal and intrigue, not battle, that gave the invaders free passage into China. The Manchus reigned as the Ching dynasty until 1912.

Placating the Barbarians

The marauding tribes were bold enough to attack ancient cities and capitals such as Loyang and Chang'an. The Wall proved deficient, and barbarians were able to break through. Advisers to the Chinese emperors had to devise more plans.

A system of bribery was the first such plan. Gold, silver, tea, fine porcelain and finally silk were all used to pay off the nomadic tribes. Then it was learnt that some nomadic chiefs had a liking for the more delicate Chinese women, carrying some away in their raids. Many women were known to have killed themselves rather than submit to the rough, uncouth men of the Steppes. The emperors' advisers began counselling them to send Chinese princesses, borne by the numerous royal concubines, to purchase peace. Dispatched too were acclaimed beauties and other ladies.

One such case was that of Wang Zhaojun, one of the four great beauties of China. It was said that she refused to bribe the artist who painted the portraits of ladies presented to the Han emperor for his selection, and, consequently, he made no attempt to capture her beauty. Wang Zhaojun was not chosen by the Emperor, and when he finally saw her in person it was too late. She had been promised to Chanyu Huhanye of the powerful Xiongnu tribes. The Han emperor was advised to let her go, as the vengeance of the Xiongnu would be too terrible to contemplate! This was in 33 BC.

The scene of Wang Zhaojun as she left for the grasslands, seated on a horse and plucking a sad tune on her lute, the pipa, has been written about by poets and painted by artists. It was said that a flock of geese flying above was so stunned by her beauty and sadness that they forgot to flap theirs wings and fell to the ground!

The City of Jian'an

This is the early fifteenth century and the powerful Ming dynasty rules China. The Great Wall is being reinforced and communications vastly improved. Beijing knows what is happening in every corner of the empire. The foreign Yuan dynasty has been overthrown and the Mongols are no longer a national threat.

The city of Jian'an, meaning healthy peace, is a fast-growing young city. Situated to the south-east of Beijing, but also not too far from Xian, it is well-placed. As a frontier town not far from the Steppes, the grasslands where the Mongol tribes roam, it has a fortress guarded by Ming troops. It is not a large army, as that is not necessary.

The first Ming emperor, Zhu Yuanzhang, had made Nanjing his capital, but his son, the Emperor Yongle, moved the capital north to Beijing. China was felt to be safe once more. As a prince, Yongle had taken part in many battles against the various tribes out in the Steppes. Many princes had been appointed commanders of the Ming armies and had seen action on the north-eastern grasslands. The early Ming rulers were only too aware of the roaming tribes and the need for a large, strong and well-trained army. Indeed, just outside Beijing was stationed such a defence force.

With secure borders Jian'an grows steadily, and many rich and powerful families choose to leave Beijing to live there. Besides, Jian'an is only a day's travel on horseback, while it is almost three days from Xian. Jian'an also has a beautiful lake comparable to that of Hangzhou, and hot springs baths that are also becoming well-known.

One household that moved there from Beijing is the Soong family, taking with them a young daughter, XiXi, who is to become the mother of Yiling, the heroine of our story.

Two generations beforehand, the Mongol tribe to which a young man called Tolui belonged roamed the nearby Steppes. After sixteen years as a nomad, the vicissitudes of life decide that Tolui should spend the rest of his life in Jian'an. He is grandfather of Hoong, the eunuch warrior, and so our story unfolds.

4

The Story of Tolui

How did a Mongol youth become a Ming warrior in China? How did his grandson become a Ming general and the hero of this story?

It was a cold wintry morning when Tolui made his entry into the world from the warmth of his mother's womb into the chill of the Steppes. As he did so he gave a robust yell as if in protest. His father, who had stood by his wife through her labour, took the infant from the midwife and raised him into the air with a loud cheer. A healthy male child!

Tolui's father was a proud young man. He loved his wife and now they had their firstborn. What was there not to be happy about?

The day before the young father and other warriors from the tribe had successfully raided a Chinese village at the border. They had brought back cattle to enlarge their stocks, grain to feed the tribe and blankets to keep themselves warm. Life was good and there was much to look forward to now that he was also a father.

When Tolui was born the Mongol Yuan dynasty had only recently been replaced in China by the Ming. Tolui belonged to one of the more isolated Mongol tribes that chose to remain independent. But they had heard of Genghis Khan and his great victories. In fact, Tolui was named after one of the sons of the great khan. Perhaps the sky god would smile kindly on the Mongols and make them powerful again. Who knows? Tolui had a birthmark on his neck shaped like a lotus.

9

An elderly member of the tribe called it a good omen, claiming that it was a sign of a good warrior. Perhaps Tolui would become a great warrior!

But Tolui did not enjoy the good fortune hoped for on the Steppes.

His first year passed peacefully enough. The child thrived on the plentiful supply of his young mother's milk. He also inherited his mother's colouring, which was fair by Mongol standards. Tolui passed all the usual milestones on time, crawled, walked and spoke. He gave no problems but problems came to the happy family.

Like other Mongol females, Tolui's mother was physically active, but when he was two she slipped in the snow carrying a load of logs and suffered a bad miscarriage. Although young she never recovered her strength.

In his third year Tolui's father was killed in battle against another tribe. It was said that his mother never smiled again, but that she kept going only because of her love for her son.

When Tolui turned five his mother passed away and he was left an orphan. The parents of his close playmate and cousin Arik took him in and brought him up.

Tolui was happy as long as Arik was around him. Arik was two years older, kind and affectionate. It was Arik who dried Tolui's tears when his pet wolf cub died. With his shorter legs, Tolui was always running after Arik, trying desperately not to lose sight of him. And so the boys grew healthy and strong.

The tribe moved often, looking for good pasture for their animals. Tolui and Arik were happy boys. In good weather they were always out on the grassland chasing each other, flying kites and looking for rabbits and squirrels. When they were deemed strong enough they were taught to ride by Arik's father. This was followed by lessons on handling the bow and arrow.

The growing boys looked forward to the feast nights in summer, when they were allowed to stay up late. Out on the Steppes there was often a cool breeze and the dark sky was studded with thousands of stars. The tribesmen would light up the area with torches, and there was the wonderful smell of meat cooking on hot stones. The Mongol men were good dancers and everyone would move to the drums and flutes, for the tribal dances were popular. Even in winter there was the occasional festival, and all except the old and sickly enjoyed the cold air.

Tolui and Arik loved their lives out on the Steppes. The crisp, cold air was part of its beauty. On some nights in their ger they would wake to the howling of wolves, but it was the thundering of the hooves of wild horses that the boys loved to hear. They would rush to catch a glimpse of the horses disappearing into the distance. In early spring Arik would take Tolui to the waterfall and pools of melted snow to bathe. Tolui had protested at first, but soon succumbed to the freshness of the cold water that left their skin tingling!

Spring was a magical time for the boys. Their activities included days watching falconry. There were a few older men who managed the falcons expertly. The pair witnessed the fearful-looking birds with equally fearful-looking eyes soar into the sky. A dive into the bushes to emerge with a rabbit. Fascinated, they watched with open mouths. And finally, what they loved most, the archery competitions.

Both Arik and Tolui excelled at archery. Arik did not seem to mind when Tolui replaced him as the champion at the age of fifteen. Both of them improved their horsemanship, learning to ride side-saddle, to shoot from a moving horse, in short to act as a single unit.

Arik's parents gave the boys the care they needed, but what was more important was their independence. The parents also had other duties and other children to look after. Their tribe's isolation meant greater autonomy, as they did not have to submit to the demands and rules of the larger groups. The disadvantage was fewer men and thus less fighting power. There were times when Tolui's tribe was short of meat and grain. At such times they had to plan and execute quick raids on the frontier cities, and at sixteen Tolui was ready for such an attack. The decision his uncle made was to change his whole life.

The tribal leaders decided that Jian'an was to be the target. Jian'an was not protected by a large army. Besides, this was a raid for supplies, not a prolonged war. It was a "hit and run".

The Mongol tribal leaders weighed their odds. Jian'an was rich and the potential rewards great. Tall, handsome Tolui was given his instructions the night before. The element of surprise was to be their advantage. They would head for the granaries and livestock, taking what they could. A small number of men was to plunder the mansions for whatever wealth they could find: silver, gold, jewellery, antiques. Speed was important. The raiding party would race through the city and head back as soon as they got their hands on what they wanted. They were to be gone before the Chinese citizens realised what had happened. The instructions were to keep moving, for those who did not would be left behind and lose their lives!

Tolui was beside himself with excitement, although he did sleep for some hours and was fresh for the raid. That he broke the cardinal rule on the need to keep moving meant the end of his life as a nomadic tribesman.

As dawn broke, Tolui and Arik charged down to the gates of the fortress. The Ming soldiers on guard were taken by surprise and the Mongols broke through the gates. Arik was among those in the lead now, with Tolui behind him, as they rode into the city.

It was also Arik's first raid. He had been disappointed when they left him out of the last raid on a small town. The colourful shops and wide streets of Jian'an dazzled him, and he stood up on his horse for a better view. Was it a dog that ran across in front of him? His horse reared and Arik fell. Tolui saw it all. The other Mongol warriors rode on. Tolui could not. It was his beloved cousin. He had to turn back. He got off his horse and rushed to Arik. Arik was hurt and his horse had bolted. Tolui helped him up and loaded him onto his own horse. Tolui was going to ride back with Arik. That was all Tolui wanted, not the spoils of the raid.

Unfortunately, the first Ming soldiers on the scene ran into the two youths. Valuable time had been lost and they were surrounded. Escape was not possible. They were indeed unfortunate, for the raid was not over. Had the young men not run into the soldiers they could have escaped. By the time the Ming troops were organised the other Mongol warriors were gone.

The raid had gone according to plan except that Arik and Tolui had been left behind!

Arik and Tolui were dragged and thrown before Commander Whang.

Arik was never going to be a slave of the Chinese. He was a proud Mongol warrior. If he could not be free he would rather die. He and Tolui had been beaten by the soldiers and now the commander was questioning them. Arik reached for the dagger hidden in his boot. In the next moment he drove it into his heart and so ended his life.

5

The Transformation of Tolui

Tolui's cousin Arik had killed himself rather than submit to the Chinese. In anguish, Tolui wanted to do the same. Why did he not kill himself or attempt to escape? Commander Whang of the fortress at Jian'an made the difference and influenced Tolui's thinking.

Commander Whang was a most unusual person for his beliefs, if nothing else. Many Chinese thinkers believed that in this mortal life there are souls whose lives are intertwined. The first time Whang saw Tolui this strong belief overwhelmed him. Tolui must not be allowed to die, for if he did Whang's life would end too! And this came true, for months later Tolui saved Whang from a Jurchen attack.

The soldiers expected to enjoy beating Tolui to death. Instead, they had strict orders to keep him alive. He was to have his wounds treated, to be fed and rested and, when he was well enough, to be presented to the commander again.

It was a dejected Tolui who greeted the Commander. Whang had seen this before. The last time was when one of two soldier brothers died in battle only a year ago. The younger brother had lost his anchor and the desire to live when the elder brother died. It was no surprise when he was found to have died by suicide. Whang was not going to let that happen with Tolui. He was going to practise patience. He was going to do what his hero, the legendary General Yue Fei of the Song dynasty did, he was going to show compassion and understanding.

Perhaps Tolui could sense that Whang meant him no harm and had concern for his welfare. And Tolui was a survivor. He did think of escape, but knew that would be difficult and it could easily end in his death. Besides he was well-guarded and where could he escape to? His tribe was too weak to take on the Ming forces at Jian'an, and he had no contact with them. Would they even know he was still alive?

Each day Tolui was sent to the Commander's room in the fortress. Whang's hobby was art. He loved to paint and allowed Tolui to watch him paint and practise calligraphy. He played the flute. Tolui could not resist the haunting tunes the Commander played. They were the love songs that Whang's wife had played to him. She had departed many years ago while still young. He had taken concubines, as was expected of him, but he still missed her.

Whang questioned Tolui about his life. Slowly Tolui began to talk about his love for the Steppes, his eyes lighting up whenever he spoke of the grasslands. The Commander knew that Tolui was mending, seeing his desire to live was strong.

One day the Commander sent for him to report in haste, for there was important news! It was news that would bring him unbearable sorrow.

There had been an outbreak of war among the Mongol tribes. Those that did not join the latest alliance were threatened with death by the stronger tribes. Tolui's tribe had defied the alliance and was used as an example. The whole tribe was massacred. Was it true? How did the Commander know for sure?

Tolui was taken to see a badly wounded man found near the fortress. Tolui recognised him. They had played together as children. He stammered out that Tolui's uncle and family had been killed. His loved ones were gone. And all the other people he knew. Who was there to go back to? In his despair, Tolui made the ultimate decision to throw in his lot with the Chinese.

Whang persuaded Tolui to show him his skills. For a sixteen year old Tolui excelled in horse riding, archery and swordsmanship. His mentor was to learn that Tolui was a good battle strategist. Whang was reminded that Tolui was still a barbarian but considered the risk of training Tolui to be his assistant worth taking.

Whang soon started asking Tolui for his thoughts on how the Ming army could be improved. He was not surprised to learn that Tolui felt the archers could do with improvement. By now the two men trusted each other. Tolui asked for twenty young men who he could train as archers. Tolui wanted new recruits and the freedom to train them with no interference from the senior Ming army officers. Whang agreed and watched what Tolui did.

Firstly Tolui selected from the many who applied. There were weeks of strengthening exercises, followed by horse riding lessons and only then archery. Slowly the motley lot became a disciplined corps that showed great promise. Whang agreed to a second group to be trained as archers, and again Tolui did not disappoint.

Tolui knew that it was too ambitious to transform the recruits to horseback archers in a matter of months, but it was possible to have good archers to shoot from the fortress walls. No invading army would be able to storm the walls unimpeded. New technology with the bow and arrow had been developed. There was greater flexibility with the bow and more deadly arrowheads. The distance that arrows travelled had also increased.

Tolui worked on uniformity with his archers. Each morning he made them shoot from the fortress walls. He rode out with his favourite men, ostensibly to retrieve the arrowheads, but really to check the distance and consistency. Meanwhile, the Commander kept the cavalry and foot soldiers well exercised, fit and alert.

And so the days passed. Not lazy, complacent days, although the Mongols in the north had been badly defeated by the Ming armies, while the Uyghurs in the west seemed quiet. For spies brought news that there was a gathering of Jurchen tribes in the north-east.

Word came from Beijing that the Jurchen tribes were to be routed. Beijing would be sending out a strong army to Jian'an to this end.

The Jurchens struck first, appearing out of the dawn haze, riding fast towards the gates of the Jian'an fortress. Their sudden appearance and their speed left the Commander with little time. His cavalry and foot soldiers emerged from the gates to battle the Jurchens. Tolui's orders were to wait for the Commander's signal. His archers lined the fortress, waiting for Tolui's orders to shoot. Tolui and his mobile archers would stay hidden initially, then make a sudden attack from the western end. That was the battle plan.

However, the Jurchens also had their plans. Isolate and capture the Chinese leader, gaining a bargaining chip. It was simple but effective. Commander Whang charged into the tribal horsemen, knocking over the first opponent and thrusting his sword into another. The next thing he knew he was grabbed by a Jurchen horseman and transferred to a second horseman. The second horseman turned around to ride back towards the Steppes.

Tolui's keen eyes saw what was happening as he waited on his horse. He shot forward, urging his willing stallion to greater speed and in no time was among the fighting men. He made his way to Commander Whang, wrenched him from the Jurchen warrior, and sped back to the fortress gates. It was an unbelievable scene. By the time the Jurchen fighters were given orders to chase them Tolui was already well away.

The fortress guards were alert, as were the archers at the walls. It did not take long for Tolui and Whang to get close. Tolui signalled his archers. The Jurchen horsemen warriors were mowed down by unfailing arrows. Tolui and the Commander reached the gates and rode through. A second flight of arrows landed on more pursuers. Still more arrows flew and more fighters fell until orders to turn back reached them. Meanwhile, the Ming cavalry did well too. From the city walls could be seen large numbers of dead or fleeing Jurchen tribesmen. These latter men met greater misfortune, for they were met by the embrace of the Ming reinforcement troops from Beijing. The Jurchens were completely defeated. It took a century for them to rebuild and reappear as the Manchus in 1644.

The fame of Commander Whang and Tolui spread far and wide. But for the courage of Tolui, it was doubtful that either Whang or the city of Jian'an would have survived.

The older commander and the young Mongol warrior were often seen together. Their partnership ensured peace for Jian'an over the following decade.

Meanwhile, Tolui learnt to appreciate Chinese culture. He wore Chinese clothes except for when he rode. Then it was Mongolian pantaloons and a loose shirt. He ate Chinese food, listened to Chinese music, and watched Chinese opera with the Commander. His Chinese archers and soldiers loved him and would die for him in battle. Tolui had taken an oath to serve the Chinese emperor and he would never betray China, but he knew that deep within him he was still Mongol.

A humble man, Tolui knew there would always be those who saw him as a barbarian and be suspicious of him. Tolui kept company with Commander Whang but made no attempt to ingratiate himself with others in the Chinese society. As a youth, he had gone to search for a partner to satisfy his needs in Jian'an's Mongol community. He found someone compatible and she gave him two children. He was in his early twenties when she died. Needing a mother for his children, he took another Mongol woman, who bore him another two children. By his mid-twenties Tolui was sufficiently affluent to own enough property to house his partner and children and an outhouse for his servants.

However, Tolui was not to live out his life quietly, for goddess Kuan Yin had good things in store for him. Having become a regular visitor to Commander Whang's mansion, he could sense a pair of eyes watching him each time he was there.

Then one day Tolui heard a slight sound behind him. He moved towards the sound while pretending to be studying the flowering bushes and caught someone by their small wrist. The owner of a pair of unusually large dark eyes. Tolui knew these were the eyes that always watched him. They belonged to an eight year old girl. She stepped forwards and said 'I am Yanni, daughter of Commander Whang', then turned and ran off.

A few more years passed. One day Tolui saw the slight figure of a young Chinese lady emerge from the bushes. She smiled at him. He knew who she was, for the dark eyes were the same. The child had grown. Her figure was lithe and graceful. She was indeed attractive. Tolui gave a sigh.

Yanni

Commander Whang was an unusual person, one who chose to think well of others. He looked for outstanding qualities in a person, not at their skin colour. That Tolui was a dark-skinned Mongol and a barbarian was not what he saw, but a talented handsome youth with much potential. Tolui, in turn, saw Whang as an uncle who accepted and trusted him. There was respect between the two men, and their concern and deep affection for the other grew as they worked and fought together.

Whang was not blind to Yanni's interest in Tolui, as she always seemed to be around when Tolui visited. Yanni was the child of the younger of Whang's two concubines, and was doted on from the time she was born. She had arrived when Whang thought he had already passed the years when he could sire a child. Yanni's mother was not considered to be young either. The pregnancy had caught everyone by surprise. Whang had a son and daughter by the senior concubine and another son from Yanni's mother. Both the sons had good jobs in the bureaucracy and the daughter married well. All three lived in Beijing.

Whang had his own love story. He was from a reputable family. His marriage was arranged, but the two young people subsequently fell in love. Whang's wife turned out to be a talented musician. She played the pipa, the Guqin and the flute, and from her Whang learned to play the flute. It was from her, too, that he learnt to appreciate the Chinese opera. The downside was her poor health. She passed away some three years after their marriage, having had one miscarriage and no live births.

Whang grieved, feeling that happiness had been snatched from him. Loneliness and a sense of duty made him accept the two concubines his older relatives selected for him. He did not want to go through the marriage rites again. One wife who he loved dearly was enough. Yet he found that there was so much love left in him when Yanni came into his life. When Whang carried her in his arms she had looked at him with those large dark eyes as if she knew he was her father. The child responded to him. From the time she was a baby, Yanni preferred him, not her mother or the nursemaid. Her chubby fingers always reached for him. When she learnt to crawl it was to her father she went. When she learnt to walk and run, it was always Whang she ran to. Whenever Whang came home from the fortress, within minutes the child was in his arms.

Yanni turned thirteen, exceptionally pretty, slim and delicate. She had escaped foot binding, for Whang could not bear for her to suffer and had said no. In any case, Yanni had rather small feet, which Whang felt were pretty enough. Her mother followed the father's wishes, for she had no strong views of her own.

When Yanni had her first bleeding, her mother went to Whang to inform him that she was ready for marriage. Whang sent for his daughter. It was a gentle scene that unfolded, no admonitions, orders or demands. Whang held his daughter's hand and asked her thoughts on marriage. Was she ready for it? Was there someone who she liked?

Yanni broke into tears and poured out her heart to her father.

She confessed that there was only one man she was ever interested in since she spotted him in their garden. She had carried the image of him in her heart since he had flashed his white teeth and his smile at her when she was eight! If she was not allowed to marry him she would become a nun and spend her life at the Buddhist temple nearby. If she was forced to marry another she would kill herself! Whang's suspicions about Yanni were correct.

Whang had also seen something else the last time Tolui was in his home. What was interesting was the look on Tolui's face as he watched the disappearing figure of Yanni. He wore this wistful, sad, but longing look. Whang felt he also had such a look for his loved one long ago. So Tolui loved Yanni too!

Whang summoned them both to a meeting. In Yanni's presence, he asked Tolui whether he would like to marry his daughter. Unable to suppress her joy, Yanni threw herself at her father, kissing him all over his face. Then unashamedly she threw herself at Tolui, doing the same. Whang knew he had done the right thing, for he could see the love between them. They were the two people most dear to him: his beloved daughter and the man who had risked his life for him. He also owed his fame and good fortune to Tolui, for everyone in Jian'an knew of the great commander and his assistant!

The day came and the couple went through the Chinese wedding rites. Both were dressed in red. As Tolui lifted her veil, Yanni thought she had married the most handsome man in the world. Tolui believed himself to be the luckiest man alive to be loved by this unmatched Chinese beauty.

Tolui felt he lived a dream for the duration of his marriage. Yanni was everything he wanted in a woman. She was the first to greet him when he came home from the fortress. She insisted on serving him herself with hot tea, soup or a delicious herbal drink. Her strong firm hands would knead his weary body and her scalp massage always brought him sleep. He loved the way her hands would run over his face and the way she buried her face in his chest. Yanni was one of a kind. Chinese females were often afraid of the hairy barbarians, covering their eyes when they accidentally ran into one!

Yanni was well loved. Rejoicing in the household was great when, a year later, a boy was born. Yue had Tolui's features but Yanni's fair complexion. In nature he was more like his mother. He inherited his father's skill in archery and horsemanship but he enjoyed studying, art and calligraphy. Yue lacked his father's toughness, but Tolui loved him dearly, as he was so much like his mother. Father and son missed

Yanni badly after she died. However, Tolui could not complain, for he had sixteen years of bliss.

Tolui watched Yue grow. Yue received the commission of captain in the Ming army and worked at the fortress. It was no surprise when Yue told Tolui he had fallen in love with a Chinese maiden named Yin. She came from a Chinese scholar's family that had fallen on hard times. She became an orphan as a teenager and her uncle was happy to be rid of her. In the uncle's view, the boy was a barbarian to whom he would not have married his own daughter, but the father-in-law was a somebody in Jian'an!

Yue was a simple happy person, and was content in his position as captain. There was peace in the country. And now, most of all, he had a wife he loved dearly.

After a year of marriage they had a son who grandfather Tolui named Hoong. They all lived happily in Tolui's large mansion in Jian'an.

6

Tolui and the Silk Road

By the time of the wedding of Tolui and Yanni, Tolui had become well known not only in Jian'an, but also in Xian. A letter came from the Governor at Xian asking that Tolui urgently be sent to Xian, for there were some problems relating to the northern trade routes, the Silk Road.

Xian was the starting point for the Silk Road and where many powerful and rich merchants lived. The city had grown rich from trade and while the Silk Road was slowly being replaced by new sea trade routes, it was still an important part of the East-West economy. The merchants demanded more security from the authorities. Of late, many caravans had been attacked by raiding tribes not far from Xian, leaving the merchants with heavy losses.

Tolui called for the merchants to meet with him.

His advice: the merchants should join forces, no fewer than ten caravans travelling together. With combined funds they could employ guards to ward off the minor attacks. Guards at the beginning, middle and end of the caravans. Tolui suggested employing tribesmen as guards as well, so they could negotiate with the larger groups of tribesmen rather than risk being slaughtered and losing everything. The attackers could be paid off. The merchants learnt to compromise.

It was a successful trip to Xian. Thereafter, many strange dark skinned bearded and turbaned men could be seen visiting Tolui at Jian'an to seek his advice.

The Gu Family — The story of Yiling and Her Parents

Yiling was a most happy child, for she was surrounded by love. Mother XiXi was always there. Her earliest memories of her mother were those of a beautiful, gentle face looking down at her with great tenderness, kissing her little fingers and toes. Behind her stood a handsome man who reached down to touch her with one hand while his other arm was around the woman he cherished.

It was Yiling's nursemaid, SuSu, who told Yiling of her parents' love story years later.

Shan was unusually handsome, with females from near and far swooning over him by the time he was fifteen. The Gu family was wealthy and established. Shan had so many talents, both physical and intellectual. As a young child he showed an enthusiasm for learning and then for sport. He was a horseman, became an expert swordsman and developed a love for archery. He grew tall and muscular. Shan was the child every parent wished for. His parents watched him grow with much happiness. Unfortunately, they perished when their carriage fell off the mountain after the horses bolted for some reason. The remains of Shan's parents were brought home for burial.

Sixteen year old Shan was inconsolable and grieved deeply for months. A younger brother of his father, Teck, helped him through the difficult time. Uncle Teck was worldly-wise. He could see that the youth had reached manhood. A few months later Teck presented Shan with two concubines and encouraged him to let them please him.

Shan was no monk and he learnt early to enjoy women. However he showed no interest in marriage. Many good-looking girls from rich and powerful families approached Teck for a match up but Shan could not be persuaded.

It appeared that Shan was waiting for someone special. Then one day he saw XiXi and his waiting came to an end.

XiXi was brought up by her grandfather, Po, as her parents had died shortly after she was born. XiXi had been protected and hidden away by her grandfather. The Soong family to which Po belonged was connected to the imperial family. They had helped the Ming founder, Zhu Yuanzhang, come to power and was rewarded with the gift of land in Beijing and a royal princess when the Emperor became well-established. That princess became Po's mother. From her, Po learnt of the intrigues of the inner palace: the pettiness and vindictiveness of the women within the harem, the malice and bitterness of the court eunuchs who felt they had been robbed of their treasures and were bent on hurting others.

Po had been devastated when his only son died unexpectedly. The death of his daughter-in-law was the final straw. He took his three year old granddaughter and moved from Beijing to Jian'an.

Po was a scholar and a poet. His favourite pastime was reading the Tang poets Wang Wei, Li Bai and Tu Fu. Then Po was in a world of his own, but his granddaughter brought him much happiness. The toddler often woke Po from naps in his study. She would climb on his lap and kiss his forehead, nose and cheeks. Her eyes, always intense, would gaze deeply into his. How could he not protect and love this child?

As XiXi grew he could see the beauty in her, the dimples at the sides of her lips, large eyes, heart-shaped face and warm smile. There had been comments about her looks by those who saw her. An old family friend, together with a neighbour, had compared her to Xi Shi (Shi Yiguang), one of the four great beauties of China. The legend said that when Xi Shi came to wash clothes at the riverside, the fish would race away to hide as Xi Shi's beauty was incomparable.

Grandfather Po protected XiXi, minimising her public activities, but he could not refuse to attend extended family reunions to honour the ancestors. XiXi met many young men at those dinners. They flocked to her side but she had no interest in any of them. However, it was at such a gathering that she met Shan. Shan was no relative, but a guest spending a few days with one of Po's cousins. The attraction was immediate and not lost on Po. Grandfather perceived a glow in

XiXi that was not there before. All too soon the elders from Shan's family came to see him, proposing marriage. The romantic poet in Po recognised that Shan and XiXi were meant to be together and felt his job was done. He was happy to hand her over in marriage. There was much fanfare and the marriage took place.

Yiling was born ten months later.

The moment Yiling started to walk she was everywhere. Then she started to run and no one could stop her. There were many falls but few tears. By the time Yiling was four none of the housemaids could catch her. Life became physically exhausting for the housemaids, but they were also devoted to the lively child. Yiling often told her mother she was born to run and that she had magic feet! XiXi would look sad, as she had to decide whether Yiling was to have her feet bound. This has become a custom amongst wealthy families, not just those of higher social standing. These families could easily afford the maids and other servants to perform the duties an unfettered female would normally do.

Foot binding – an important aside

XiXi herself had escaped foot binding. There was not the usual pressure from family womenfolk, since Po was something of a recluse. Besides, he would not have allowed his beloved granddaughter to be subjected to so much pain! Women blindly followed the customs to which they themselves had been subjected. The painful, debilitating, sometimes deadly, practice had even started spreading to lower class families.

The superficial values: the belief that "lotus feet" brought delight to men and social prestige to the family. Or was there a hidden motive as well? It kept the wife virtuous, as she was a prisoner at home. She could not run away. For poorer families, it might enable them to sell a girl-child into a higher status family, thereby enriching themselves, or tie her to the home to make handicrafts and earn an income for the family. There were stories of large-footed girls who ran away with their lovers and women who rebelled against the beatings of violent or drunken husbands. The stay-at-home wife had one man, while he could roam and have many women, especially if he was wealthy. Down through the centuries Han women undermined their own kind and championed the rights of their sons to do as they pleased.

Even Yiling's nursemaid, SuSu, had been an indirect victim of foot binding.

When Yiling was just three, SuSu was given permission for a long break to visit her family in a village some distance away. SuSu had gone in high spirits, for it was to be a reunion with her own little daughter. SuSu's woodcutter husband had died four years before, crushed by a falling tree, leaving her with an infant daughter. The child, named Lan, was a gift left by him rather than a reminder of the pain of his loss. However, as a result, SuSu needed to work and was hired by Shan to be nursemaid to Yiling. SuSu left Lan to be raised by her capable older sister-in-law.

In three days SuSu was back, barely recognisable. Her face was swollen from crying and she could hardly stand. That night Yiling crept into SuSu's room. SuSu was lying in bed, her eyes closed but with tears seeping out. It was Yiling's first experience of grief. She could often make SuSu laugh but now she was utterly helpless. Yiling could do nothing for SuSu.

Yiling eventually learnt from her mother that little Lan had died.

Unbeknownst to SuSu, the aunt raising her had passed away the previous year. Lan had been sent to a foot binder by an unscrupulous second aunt who thought she could profit from making a child bride of Lan. However, infection from inexpert cleaning and care of Lan's feet, plus poor nutrition, had brought death to the young girl. SuSu was not going to be told but duped into the continued remittance of money!

Although Yiling was only a child she was now aware of sadness and pain. The practice of foot binding was the cause. These thoughts were to haunt Yiling for the rest of her life.

The Gu Family continued

But back to the happy little family. When Yiling was five she was allowed to sit with her mother to watch her father practise his swordsmanship in their large rear courtyard.

Father Shan had a superb body and his moves, agility and sword poses were things of beauty. Mama XiXi loved watching while Father enjoyed her admiration. He always displayed his best whenever she was watching. When he finished Mama would play sweet and gentle music on the Guqin, an instrument at which she excelled. Father would slip onto the bench next to her and also start plucking at the strings. Together they would play a duet.

When they finished there was always the sound of soft clapping from a pair of small hands, and the sound of a child laughing in glee. These were treasured memories that Yiling stored away in her mind.

Life was good, like a dream. There was always the three of them and they needed no one else. Sometimes Mama would play the pipa with a faraway look, for the tunes from the pipa always seem sad.

Father also had a serious side, and could spent hours reading or practising calligraphy. Mama would be seated close by, painting her favourite flowers, the peony or plum blossoms.

Yiling loved her mother's paintings of winter scenes of the snow on the trees and houses. If the child was bored she would run off to play "catch me" with the maids. She was rarely caught!

Pesky Uncle Teck would visit every month. Shan respected him and felt he was always helpful.

Teck tried to persuade Shan to mix socially, but he had a hidden agenda. Shan had no male heirs. Teck believed this problem could be solved if Shan took concubines. Years before Shan had accepted the two concubines his uncle had gifted him but sent them away long ago. Shan only had eyes for XiXi from the moment he saw her.

Yiling was in her sixth year when her parents took her to a large reunion of the Gu family. Although Yiling did not have the beauty, dimples or heart-shaped face of XiXi, she still stood out. She did, however, have that beautiful smile which was later to beguile Hoong.

Yiling was amazed to find that she had so many cousins. She found herself intimidated by so many pairs of eyes on her. Then she heard the "whispered" remarks about her. 'She is not as pretty as her mother. Besides look at her large feet! Who would want to marry her?'

Yiling darted towards her mother, but a woman suddenly crossed her path. There was the slightest brush, more wind generated by movement. In the next moment there was a scream and the woman fell, toppling on her small feet and falling heavily. It was the wife of Shan's cousin. Suddenly the bored women had more than gossip to think of. They all rushed to help her while someone shouted that a child had knocked her over! The shrill voices travelled to the next room where the men were. It was customary for the men to be talking politics or business in another room, away from the women, at such gatherings. The men came in to investigate the commotion. Father Shan shot through. He swept up a teary Yiling with one arm and had the other protectively round XiXi. He was a picture of love for his two females. XiXi had been apologising profusely to the "fallen" lady.

Shan, on learning that Yiling had been implicated, apologised.

Father's cousin Cheng stepped forward. He addressed his now seated, fully recovered wife, Lady Ee.

'You have fallen again. How many times do l have to tell you never to move about without the maid's help?' Shan apologised to his cousin, who was fair and courteous. 'My wife is known to be careless and your daughter is only a child. It is an accident, speak no more of it.'

As Yiling sat with her mother, an older cousin, May, approached the still mortified Yiling and warmly grasped her hands. She asked XiXi and Yiling to follow her to the pond in the back garden where they could admire the goldfish. They had to walk slowly, for cousin May had bound feet. Out came the story of Lady Ee, the lady with the smallest feet in the city of Jian'an.

Lady Ee's mother was very ambitious, sending for the best-known foot binder in the city when Ee was only five. The mother could see Ee would never be a beauty, having her father's coarse features. For the next few years it was a noisy household, with a crying child and a shouting mother. The foot binding was successful, as the expert binder was hygienic and aware of the dangers of infection. It was an extremely satisfied mother as news spread that her daughter had the smallest feet. Lady Ee's fame spread and proposals of marriage came, although any marriage would only take place after her first "bleeding".

Cheng was not interested in Ee, having seen another, but the pressure from his parents was too great. His father ordered Cheng to obey his mother. So that was decided. Cheng's mother wanted a daughter-in-law with the smallest feet in the city. She would be one-up on all her friends and enemies. Cheng was not happy, but Ee was most contented with her life. She had married into wealth and had sons and daughters. She had done her duty. That her husband did not love her mattered little; he had fathered her children. She was full of herself. After all, she was the lady with the smallest feet in the city. And, in the end, Cheng managed to bring his childhood sweetheart into the family as a concubine and enjoyed some measure of happiness. That was the story cousin May told XiXi and Yiling.

May also told them that her feet still gave her pain, even though the binding process had been completed. She also said she hated the smell when she took off the bindings each night. May said she envied Yiling and wished she had normal feet. (Years later Yiling learnt that May had died of infection. The smell was a warning sign.)

XiXi was in deep thought after that night. She knew that Yiling loved to run. She was becoming convinced that Yiling should not be forced to have her feet bound. Anyway, she did not need to make the decision until Yiling was eight years of age.

Yiling was seven when XiXi found she was pregnant again. Father Shan was overjoyed, as was Yiling, who wanted a sibling to play with, cuddle and love. Mama XiXi told Yiling she had always wanted a girl first. This time XiXi was convinced it would be a boy. She was happy for Shan to have a male heir to continue the family line.

At the end of the fourth month XiXi fell and began to bleed. Shan ordered complete bed rest. Both he and Yiling sat with her each day. The bleeding stopped and things returned to normal. Shan was back at his morning sword practice with his wife and daughter watching. XiXi returned to playing the Guqin and pipa.

Yiling had turned eight when XiXi was but a month short of full term and suddenly started bleeding again. Shan's orders to the family doctor were 'My wife's health is most important. She comes first, even if it is at the cost of the baby!'

The baby, a boy, was born dead. XiXi was seriously ill. Shan begged her not to leave them. He had never been known to cry before, but was often in tears, and Yiling also.

XiXi hovered between life and death. She did not want to leave her husband and daughter, but would her body listen to her? She seemed to be pulling through, often gently returning the pressure that Shan applied to her fingers as he held them. However, Shan and Yiling were to learn that no matter how hard you begged, fate does not yield!

One morning the fight ended. A serene XiXi lay dead, although she appeared only to be asleep. She was as beautiful as ever. Neither Shan nor Yiling could believe that XiXi had gone.

Father and child clung together as they grieved. Uncle Teck and extended family members tried to console them, but Shan's orders were to leave him alone and no one dared interfere.

Yiling and Shan were in deep mourning. The physical changes to Shan were more noticeable. He wasted away, his eyes sunken, and he seemed to lose interest in living. The Gu family was afraid that he would join his wife before long. Yiling, now nine, was thin and had a small sad face. She was going past the feet binding age. None of the related womenfolk dared intervene for they were afraid of Shan. Why get into his bad books when there was no chance Shan would listen? And so Yiling remained free to run around on her "magic feet".

One day, after Shan fell into the deep sleep of emotional exhaustion, Yiling ran to the bamboo forest, not far away. She sat on a fallen log, sobbing, when she was startled by the appearance of a boy only a little older than her. When he tried to speak to her she got up and ran back home.

7

Tolui's Mongol Family

Tolui led a good life in Jian'an even before he married Yanni. He put all his earnings into the vast property he bought and built up. Space was what the young Mongol man wanted for himself and his family. He had a Mongol family, for as a young man Tolui had found a suitable girl from the small Mongol community in Jian'an. Tolui's first partner had given him two sons, Arik, named after Tolui's late cousin, and Burke. Unfortunately, she passed away while the boys were still young. Tolui took another Mongol woman to give them a mother and carer, as he was often away at the fortress. She gave him another son, called Batu. Tolui was kind to his partners, but never loved them like he later loved Yanni. The Mongol family lived in the west wing of Tolui's sprawling residence.

As a teenager, Arik followed Tolui to work at the fortress. Arik was a happy, simple soul, absolutely devoted to his father. When Yue was born to Tolui and Yanni, Arik was the most excited member of the family and accepted Yue as his brother. That they had different mothers mattered not at all!

Arik eventually married a girl from the Mongol community. After two miscarriages, Batir was born to the union, bringing great joy to the household. By this time Yue was a young man, and married Yin, daughter of a poor Chinese scholar. Hoong was born to Yue and Yin the following year. While Batir was fully Mongol, Hoong's mother and grandmother were Han Chinese. Due to Tolui's fairness and skill at managing people, there was no ill will and much harmony within this large household.

Tolui's second son, Burke, went to work in Xian. He did well in business. Tolui's third son, Batu, persuaded his father to allow him to join the caravaners of the Silk Road. He returned once when Hoong was seven. Hoong had stayed up listening to his uncle Batu's stories of the towns and oases across the deserts through which he journeyed. Batu had seen the wonders of Samarkand, but also told of the Mogao Caves, a treasure house of Buddhism near Dunhuang, the western-most outpost of China. In the caves at Mogao were Buddhist paintings, sculptures and scriptures. Batu told of his ambition to visit the lands beyond Central Asia. In a few months he was gone again, never to return.

Tolui was concerned about his entire family, although, of all his children and grandchildren, he loved Hoong the most. It was not merely because of his great love for Yanni. Hoong was exceptionally intelligent and attractive, with a nature to match. Batir had tried hard to dislike Hoong but failed, for the child was so loving. When Hoong started to walk he not only wandered often into Tolui's study but to the west wing as well. He was looking for Batir. When he learnt to talk, it was 'Ba…Ba… wait for little Hoong.' He would ask his Mongol uncles to carry him, looking up at them with his huge eyes and raising his arms to be lifted. He had also done this to Tolui's second Mongol partner and covered her face with kisses the first time she carried him, leaving her giggling.

Yanni, beloved wife of Tolui and mother of Yue, did her part in bringing the family together. She shared whatever she had. Every time they had an open roast of chicken or goat, Yanni made sure that one was sent to the west wing. Even the servants had a share. Yanni frequently checked that the Mongol family did not go without. Daughter-in-law Yin followed Yanni's example.

Hoong's attachment to Batir never faltered. Batir remembered the excited four year old shouting for him one afternoon outside the west wing. Hoong signalled Batir to secrecy so they went to a far corner. There Hoong revealed what he had hidden in his clothes. 'Lychees!' A small fruit Batir had seen only once before.

Lychees were found only in the south of China. Father Yue had been given two dozen. Mother Yin had shrieked in delight, for she recognised them as the sweet fruit loved by Yang Kwei Fei, the famous concubine of Emperor Xuanzong of the Tang dynasty. It was said that she so besotted the Emperor that he neglected his duties to spend time with her. He was also known to have sent countless riders to their deaths to bring lychees back to the north. The fruit had to be fresh, otherwise she would not eat them. Yang Kwei Fei was one of the four great beauties of China.

Yue gave seven of the luscious, ripe and almost bursting lychees to Hoong. Hoong had eaten two and hidden the rest away for Batir.

8

The Bamboo Forest

Many years before, a courting couple had meandered into the bamboo forest and been killed by a nest of snakes. The couple's families, enraged by their deaths, hunted down and wiped out the snakes, but the place had gained a bad reputation and was avoided by locals. It turned out to be an ideal meeting place for Hoong and Yiling.

Hoong had already been seeking refuge in the bamboo forest for a year before he saw eight year old Yiling on his favourite fallen log, sobbing. He had escaped there to grieve when Tolui died, utterly heartbroken and weeping as bitterly as he saw Yiling doing now. Grandfather had been such a tower of strength to the family after the death of Yin, Hoong's mother. Hoong found so much comfort in Tolui's craggy but still strong arms. However, Tolui passed away a year later, when, unconscious, he fell from a horse. Hoong spoke to Yiling, but she ignored him and ran off.

Tolui's residence had become a sad place. Yue was able to keep things going and the entire family remained united. Hoong continued his private Chinese, poetry and calligraphy classes, as well as his sword and kung fu practise. The latter two he did with Batir. Yue would never forget his promise to Hoong's mother. Yin always said an uneducated man was no more than an empty rice pot! Mother Yanni had only sixteen years with Yue but made him such a learned person.

It was months later when Hoong again saw the crying girl in the forest, very still and looking incredibly sad. He sat a little distance from her, unnoticed. Suddenly she gave a squeal, for a rabbit ran over her feet. Its fur was so soft and she burst into a little laugh. Hoong watched as the girl's features transformed into the most beautiful face. Fascinated, he moved closer and said hello. She turned, looked and greeted him, then got up and ran off.

Some weeks later she found Hoong seated on the log and went up to him. She brought out a big peach and handed it to him. He took a big bite, exclaiming at its sweetness. 'Yes, Mama loved them. It was her favourite fruit. Papa bought the best for her every year. But now that she has gone he won't even look at it'. He listened in silence as she prattled on. Yiling felt she could tell him everything. She told him Mama taught her to play the pipa and she would play it for him one day. Then when she finally stopped, he told her about his beloved grandfather Tolui. They found that they enjoyed confiding in each other. Yiling realised much time had passed. She jumped up and ran home before she would be missed. She did not want anyone to know of her meetings.

And so they continued to meet, their conversations ranging wide. One day Hoong arrived out of breath. He told Yiling that he had just learnt a Mongolian dance from his cousins. Hoong said that he could not move his legs as fast as his Mongol cousins, who were smaller in build, but he could fold his arms, squat and kick each leg out in turn. Yiling noticed that Hoong's legs were very long!

Spontaneously, Yiling jumped up, gracefully waving her hands and arms and whirling her body. Their movements soon synchronised and Hoong and Yiling were back-to-back as they looked over their shoulders at each other. They danced until they were exhausted and collapsed laughing on the log. Chatting again, Yiling told Hoong that Mama XiXi had said Chinese men loved dancing from ancient times. Father Shan was a good dancer, while Mama had beautiful hand movements. Yiling said she had seen her father throw her mother into the air and catch her. Hoong told Yiling that his Mongol cousins loved tribal dancing, especially at springtime, but also in winter. Both learnt that tribal men and Chinese men loved to cook.

Yiling left the forest with a sense of exhilaration. It was like the happy times when her mother was still alive. Father Shan was now thin and seemed to have no laughter in him anymore. It was more than two years since XiXi left. He no longer practised his sword play. He still read, but only sad poetry. He did not play the Guqin, just the flute, although only sad tunes. Happily, Hoong was replacing Shan and giving Yiling some joy in life.

9

—

A Sword Dance in the Bamboo Forest

Yiling turned eleven years of age. Mama XiXi was no more and Yiling would grieve forever! But she had Hoong. Father Shan had only her. The days were not as bad for Shan when he had his daughter around, but the nights without XiXi were most painful.

Shan was still overwhelmed with grief by the time a gentle smile returned to Yiling's face. Hoong was the source of her happiness. He could make her laugh. Gentle, kind Hoong. Yiling could see that Hoong was becoming very tall and even better looking!

There was something she had kept from him. She never told him that she could perform the famous sword dance, for few ladies could do it. They could not with their bound feet, nor was it easy to find someone to teach the dance, as there were so few experts.

When Yiling was five she was mesmerised by her father's sword exercises. Not long afterwards, XiXi's cousin had visited Jian'an with her opera troupe. The troupe specialised in acrobatics, but included a lady who performed the sword dance. It was the most beautiful dance Yiling had seen in her life. She begged Mama to find her a teacher.

Mama's cousin knew the sword dancer well. This had been her last performance, as she had just married, retired and, fortuitously, moved to Jian'an. That she agreed to teach Yiling was again good fortune, for she could not refuse XiXi's cousin.

Yiling started almost immediately, for her teacher said one needed agility and youth, otherwise the dancer could only be mediocre. In the first year, Yiling only learnt to move her feet and arms like that of a dancer. The next year she was taught acrobatics and how to move at speed but with little noise. Then, in the third year, her lessons were how to move and swing gracefully with the swords. XiXi had the best swordsmith in Jian'an make small, light swords for Yiling. Over the next year Yiling suddenly shot up in height, so XiXi had new swords made as well as a new costume. It was the same year that XiXi passed away.

Yiling performed her first sword dance in the year before XiXi died. She did not disappoint her parents. Afterwards, the three of them embraced with much delight at Yiling's success. Her teacher was there, and had only praise for her student. Yiling had sworn to herself that she would only do the dance for her parents, but now she wanted to do it for Hoong. Her deep affection for him was not unlike that she had for Mama. She would surprise him.

Yiling packed the swords and the dance costume and ran off to the bamboo forest. As planned, she was early and there before Hoong. She changed her shoes and into the costume, concealing herself until Hoong arrived and sat on the fallen tree trunk. Quietly, she came up to the empty space in front of where Hoong was seated. She held both swords behind her with one hand. She went up to Hoong, curtsied and paid her respects before she started her dance.

A shocked Hoong thought he was hallucinating. Before him was what he had seen in books, a fairy-like figure in striking red, yet when their eyes met the smile could only be Yiling's. Then Yiling began her dance.

She went into her first stance, one hand holding both swords, the other pointing with her second and third finger at the swords before her. Next she separated the swords, one in each hand. She twirled them and leapt into the air. Yiling swung the swords in front of her as she moved her body forwards and backwards, lower each time. She had done her best for her parents and so it was for Hoong. It had taken many years of practice to perfect, but she had loved it. She handled the swords with great agility as the glitter and flashes of reflected light created a dream-like scene.

Hoong could not take his eyes from Yiling. Was this a fantasy? This beautiful creature between child and woman, whom he adored, performing like a supernatural being. A shy humble Yiling who never told him that she could dance like this!

10

Hoong and Yiling

In the Tolui residence, the building at the back was occupied by the Mongol servants who were faithful to Tolui and loved his children. When Tolui died, son Yue told them they could stay and were never to consider leaving. Some four families were there by the time Hoong was ten years of age. Cousin Batir was the one who knew them well. Batir, who was three years older, could see Hoong's "growing pains", having gone through them himself. One evening when Hoong was fourteen, Batir took him to a small room at the far end of the servant's quarters, telling him there was something important to be done. Hoong waited while his cousin disappeared.

Hoong sensed that someone had slipped in and looked around. He saw a comely Mongol girl, Ni Ni, much older than him. He stood transfixed as he realised what was going on. She undressed him, then herself, and led him to the bed. She was experienced, he a willing novice. Hoong was physically satisfied and most grateful. Yes, the tribal people understood life so much better. No stigma was attached to young people making love. Most young couples ended up together. When they did not, any child from a union was accepted and loved by the others, especially the older womenfolk.

Hoong was unusually mature, recognising the significance of the situation. He was not being unfaithful to Yiling, as their attachment was growing ever stronger.

Afterwards, Batir had a quiet word with him, advising him to meet Ni Ni for a second time. Hoong had been feeling unsettled. He was often at the bamboo forest but Yiling did not appear the last two times. Hoong thought that Shan must be upsetting her. He had not wanted to meet Ni Ni again, but his disappointment at missing Yiling made him decide to see her just once more.

The next night Hoong made his way to the servants' quarters. As he entered the room he heard a female voice calling softly from the bed. As he approached she arose and proceeded to undress him. To Hoong's surprise he found it was a smaller but even more experienced female. She whispered 'I am Mia, and I am here to service you'.

Hoong found that females are different. Mia was more expressive. She wiggled, sighed and moaned. Hoong was certainly surprised by what happened that night. As they lay spent, another figure shot into the room. A sobbing voice called out, 'Mia you cheat, you stole Hoong from me'. Hoong was stunned and speechless. The speaker rushed out of the room while Mia remained on the bed. Mia turned to Hoong. She apologised and proceeded to explain what she had done.

Mia told Hoong that she had long loved him, even though she had a boyfriend working at the fortress. She recalled watching him with his grandfather. She noticed as he shot up in height at twelve, with shoulders broadening and muscle growing over the next year. After Batir arranged for Ni Ni to "tutor" Hoong, Mia got close to her. From Ni Ni Mia learnt that, novice though he was, Hoong had turned out to be a good lover. Besides, Hoong had an excellent body. Mia found out that there was to be a second meeting and this time she was not going to be left out. Mia schemed to make sure Ni Ni was delayed. She was lucky. Hoong was on time and Mia achieved what she wanted most in her life: some quiet moments to love Hoong.

Hoong felt he had indeed learnt the mysteries of a man's love life, but that the two liaisons were enough. He loved only Yiling.

However, a few days later Hoong bumped into Mia by what he thought was accident. Tears filled her eyes as she begged him to meet her again. She was an interesting person, pretty and delicate. And again, Yiling had not turned up at the bamboo forest. Hoong decided he would see Mia once more.

Mia knew that she was lucky to see Hoong again and that he pitied her. Hoong would have been happy to just chat, but Mia was going to take physical advantage of every moment of the short time she had with him. Hoong was not to regret the meeting, for Mia taught him how tender and gentle love could be. Still, Mia knew that Hoong meant it when he said goodbye to her. He loved someone else. Mia could only say a prayer to goddess Kwan Yin. 'Please, in my next life let me be the beloved of someone like Hoong.'

While Hoong had been initiated into manhood, Yiling remained innocent. Her old wet nurse, SuSu was still with her when XiXi died. It was from SuSu that Yiling learnt much about life. SuSu told her that men were different and less easy to satisfy than women. The first time for a girl was a very painful experience. Yiling had her first bleeding only recently but SuSu did not let Shan know. She kept Yiling's secret. The distant aunts were a vicious lot who had no love for Yiling and SuSu did not want her pushed into marriage.

Meanwhile, as father Shan and daughter Yiling grew distant from each other, Uncle Teck appeared more frequently at their house. He was afraid of losing the chance to acquire Shan's fortune!

Teck recalled that Shan accepted his offer of concubines long ago. The wily old fox would use women again. He went to the famous courtesan house in Jian'an, seeking the most attractive and experienced women. Here were courtesans who not only had looks but could play the whole range of musical instruments, as well as sing and dance. Shan rejected their initial efforts but Teck managed to get him drunk and bedded. It was a great game for the courtesans, as Shan was not only rich but handsome, even in his wasted state. The floodgates opened and Shan was interested in women once again!

The next thing Yiling knew, two attractive concubines arrived at the Gu household. Confused, she stayed home to seek an explanation from her father. For that reason she did not venture out to the bamboo forest. Each day Yiling looked for her father, but he now lived at the other end of the house and evaded her. She started to hear female tittering from the far end of the mansion and an occasional laugh in her father's voice.

Yiling, now thirteen, was determined to speak with him, no more waving her away and rushing off. She waited the whole morning until he appeared with yet another female under his arm. Yiling had heard from the servants that both his concubines were pregnant. She rushed up to him. Again he was drunk. The man gave her a cold look, waved her away and turned back to cuddle the woman.

Yiling could hardly recognise her father. Shan looked coarse and uncouth. He had put on weight and was no longer the handsome, dashing figure of the past. Could this be the same person her mother loved? Was this the devoted husband and loving father? Why was he so faithless to the memory of XiXi? How could he have changed so much? Yiling felt great pain, intense heartbreak.

Yiling fled the residence through the gate in the back garden. She ran and ran as hot tears rushed down her cheeks. When she looked up she had arrived at the bamboo forest. She thanked mother XiXi for the gift of normal feet.

She went to the fallen log. Hoong was already there. Yiling sat close to him and sobbed her heart out. He put an arm around her and let her weep as he silently shared her pain.

After almost an hour Hoong helped her up, telling her he would take her to the caves, a walk of about an hour. Hoong had been there more than once with his cousins. There was still plenty of daylight and they would be able to get back by nightfall.

The caves were interesting and would be a distraction for Yiling's unhappiness.

Fourteen year Hoong and thirteen year old Yiling found their way to the caves where Hoong and his cousins had found paintings of dancing girls. Rumour had it that these were paintings from the Tang dynasty, scenes of the imperial court, of banquets. Why they had been abandoned nobody knew! Hoong led the way to one of the larger caves.

The paintings delighted Yiling. She had been able to make out some of the fruits at the royal banquet. She spent a happy two hours there before it was time to make tracks for home. At the mouth of the caves they found it was raining lightly. They would make a run for it! As they ran the weather quickly worsened. Hoong realised the rainy season had begun and they would be better off returning to the caves and waiting it out.

By the time they got back to the caves they were both soaked. Hoong gathered some twigs, branches and leaves to start a fire. And so they resigned themselves to wait out the rain, hopefully for only a few hours.

Once Hoong got the fire going he asked Yiling to hand him her outer clothes for drying. She emerged from behind the large rock, handing Hoong her outer garments, still wearing a thin silk vest and satin leggings. Hoong was bare-chested but had on three-quarter length soft black satin pants. He told her he would not look but she came out too fast, or was it that he closed his eyes too slowly? She looked straight at him, seeing his strong wide chest was covered with a soft fuzz of fine black hair. Hers was the more provocative figure, lithe, shapely, firm. The tribal girls did not have Yiling's height or slimness. She had the most beautiful figure Hoong had ever seen.

He could neither stop moving towards Yiling nor stop himself from taking her into his arms. Yiling was frightened, yet a strange calm overtook her. She saw the tenderness on Hoong's face, but also that he wanted her. Then it happened. She bit her lip as the pain spread through her body, finally resolving itself into bliss. He cried out his love, while Yiling never wanted to be separate from him again. They fell into a dreamlike sleep. She woke. The embers from the fire still glowed and she studied his almost perfect features while he continued to slumber in her arms. He was indeed handsome.

They both slept for another couple of hours.

It was still dark when a serene Yiling woke again. She was happy to have given her virginity to Hoong. He was the person who meant the most to her in the world. Her father had spurned her and she seemed to have lost her love for him. From now on she would tell him she would marry only Hoong and no one else.

Hoong awoke with a start. The rain had stopped. He started to rise, as he had to get Yiling home, but she halted him with a touch. He could read her thoughts. She wanted him again. This time she relaxed as he entered her. They knew this time was forever and allowed the love to envelope them both.

The sky was brightening as Hoong took Yiling home, both of them feeling as if they were in a dream. Arriving at the rear of the Gu residence, Yiling knocked at the small side gate, which was opened by her faithful sleepless and anxiously waiting maid, Lin. She turned to face Hoong, handsome Hoong with his stern face. She gave him her beautiful smile, lingered for a moment then swiftly moved inside. It was to be an eternity before they would meet again.

Yiling went back to her room and gently cleaned herself. There was mild bleeding and tenderness. SuSu had said that her virginity was special, meant for one man. Yiling agreed. It was meant for Hoong, the man she loved. She slept the whole morning. Lin told SuSu and the other servants that Yiling was a little unwell and did not wish to be disturbed.

Hoong returned home in an uncharacteristically vague state, seen only by Batir. Batir knew about his meetings with Yiling in the bamboo forest, as Hoong gave himself away with his dreamy look after each innocent meeting. Batir followed him once, for he could read Hoong's face. Seeing Hoong in the early hours this time he suspected what had happened, for Hoong wore a special smile!

11

Of War and Politics in the State of Hu

China's history is one of ambition and intrigue. Cities rose against each other within China, as did sons against their fathers. There was also the problem without – that of the barbarian tribes to the north and north west. There was much for China to do!

The first Ming emperor, Zhu Yuan Zhang, was a commoner. He made Nanjing his capital, but his son, the Yongle Emperor, moved the imperial centre north to Beijing. This was the practical solution if the new dynasty wanted better control over barbarians who recognised no borders.

Jian'an's rapid development was due to its proximity to Beijing, which was closer than Xian, the start of the Silk Road. Jian'an was also closer to Beijing than Hu'xinzhou, capital of Hu, a large and sleepy hollow with an ancient history. Hu'xinzhou was only a day's march to the south of Jian'an.

The state of Hu had a special importance: it was permitted its own standing army. The governor of Hu was fiercely loyal to the Ming Emperor, but it had been some twenty years since he had raised and trained his army to fight. The Hu army had fought the tribes at the border and even eradicated the pirates who had fled inland. However, times were changing. The governor was ageing and losing his grip over the army. Even worse, he had been nursing a viper in the form of his eldest son. Loong thought his father a sickly old fool and observed the rapid growth of Jian'an and its wealth with envy.

Young Loong had cunning and patience. He had worked his way through the state army, showing ability and rising to be second-in-command. If a common nobody could establish a dynasty so could he!

Before long the governor passed away and it took Loong no time to get rid of the old advisers. Loong had spent many years working with the army and now he had control of it, creating new divisions and expanding the number of recruits. It was natural to cast covetous eyes on Jian'an.

Loong promised his soldiers and captains gold, silver and land. They would be allowed to keep what they looted, for there was so much wealth in Jian'an. But there was a note of caution. Loong told the soldiers to be selective. There may be a few powerful families who had migrated from Beijing and maintained small armies of their own. Do not touch them at all costs, Loong instructed. There were still many wealthy homes that had no guards, as Jian'an was known to be safe. The sacking was to be a quick, aggressive raid like that of the tribes on smaller Chinese cities.

The assault on Jian'an was sudden and ferocious. It brought death and change to two families in particular, those of Hoong and Yiling, within two days of the young lovers' return from the caves. Yiling was preparing to tell father Shan that she wanted to marry Hoong, while Hoong planned to ask his father to approach Yiling's father for her betrothal. They had only spent one day and night at home when the soldiers from Hu attacked at dawn.

At Yiling's house, soldiers burst in on a half-drunk Shan. He tried to protect his new concubine but was cut down before he could reach his sword. The residence was looted and torched. By good fortune, the soldiers missed Yiling's room, where she and her maid cowered fearfully. Perhaps it was because there was so much booty in Shan's room and study! Yiling and her maid managed to escape the fiercely burning building without being spotted.

Perhaps Tolui's residence should have been by-passed, for the fiercest resistance took place there. Hoong was woken by shouting from the west wing. They were being attacked! Lamps in the servants' quarters were lit as they searched for weapons to protect themselves. It was Hoong who shouted orders to use Grandfather's swords from the study. Batir and Hoong reached the study and grabbed Tolui's swords. Hoong found Tolui's favourite, which fitted well into his hand, and they ran to meet the intruders. Father Yue and his cousin had their own swords and raced to the fortress, for they had to defend Jian'an.

The two youngsters fought bravely, but they were fighting many well-trained soldiers. They were taken prisoner and marched overnight, with other captives, arriving at a large prison in Hu'xinzhou late the next morning.

Yiling was the only survivor of her family. Hoong and Batir were both wounded and prisoners. Father Yue and the Mongol uncles had been killed by the Hu soldiers. Could life be more cruel? Yes it could!

The Hu army had reduced half of the city to ruins and smoke was still rising from the burnt buildings twenty-four hours later. The new governor of Hu cast a worried eye over the ruins. His orders had left little pockets of property untouched, those of the recent migrants from Beijing with their small private armies. His first doubts arose. Should he issue them an invitation to join him? What would Beijing do when they learnt of his attack on Jian'an? Had he bitten off more than he could chew? He had been so convinced by his own ambition.

The Castration

Hoong woke from a short, troubled sleep when the prisoner next to him cried out in pain. Hoong was also in pain, for he had sustained many injuries.

The prison gate was thrown open as several soldiers entered. A small soldier came up to him. His face was full of hatred as he started kicking Hoong. He shouted to the others 'It is this young son of a whore who killed my two brothers, honourable soldiers of the state of Hu. He deserves a death more horrible than the usual'. His face twisted and covered with spittle, the soldier dragged Hoong, throwing him into a line of young boys moving out of the prison. There was much laughter as Hoong joined the queue.

Hoong was too injured to resist. There was a dozen of them in line. They were prodded towards a corner where a big man with a bare torso stood with a sharp large knife.

Hoong was dazed, his eyes hardly able to focus, but he couldn't miss the scream of pain and anguish from the boy in front of him. No one who heard it could ever forget. Hoong steeled himself, for he was next. The knife came down on his groin. It was a pain Hoong never thought possible. He fainted.

Hoong woke to cries for water from those around him. No liquids could be given for fear of complications from the brutal castrations, but there was some moisture in the thick gruel they were given.

The victims of choice were eight to ten year olds. Hoong had been in prison with the adults, and was only with the youngsters because of the venom of the Hu soldier. Castration was for the sons of rebels, murderers, political dissenters. Or those who sold their children from poverty.

The medical knowledge of the time kept open the urinary passages of the castrati, and most survived the first hundred days, after which they were sure to continue living.

Young and fit Hoong survived the cruel fate he was given. Throughout the hundred days, as he hovered between life and death, the scene of Yiling performing the sword dance in the bamboo forest had come to him. The pain of recovery made him feel like departing the world, yet time and again the scene of smiling and graceful Yiling had kept him going.

Meanwhile news of the sacking of Jian'an reached Beijing. The Emperor was enraged. Hu demonstrated how dangerous regional armies could be. No emperor could tolerate such insolence. With little delay, a large army under renowned General Wan was sent to defeat Governor Loong and restore order in both Jian'an and Hu. Too late, Governor Loong learnt he would never be allowed to get away. He chose to fight but was no match for General Wan's Ming forces.

Hoong was recovering when news reached him that the Imperial punitive forces had reached Hu'xinzhou and the state would come under General Wan. Hoong was already hobbling around when the General visited the casualties from Jian'an. He had mostly recovered from his back injuries and castration, his fine health and will to live pulling him through. His spirits and determination to survive were strengthened by the discovery that Batir still lived, even if only just. Hoong nursed Batir, feeding and comforting him.

Hoong was a very sad person in the months after his recovery in Hu'xinzhou. He heard that Tolui's large residence in Jian'an had been burnt to the ground. There was news that the Gu residence was completely razed, with no survivors. His home was gone and so too the love of his life. Each day as he cleansed himself he was reminded that he was a man no more. When Hoong was a child his mother would laughingly refer to his "treasures", but they had been hacked away. Batir told him that he looked 100% normal and no one would know his "treasures" were missing. Hoong's most precious memories were those few hours he had with Yiling in the caves. With a sigh he told himself perhaps they would meet again in the next lifetime.

The sadness showed in his eyes, and males found him intriguing and charismatic and would like him as a friend. Females found him irresistible!

General Wan's sharp eyes also noticed the unusually good looking and well-built young man when he did his rounds. The General could see there was more to him than being a good fighter.

12

Duke Wu and Yiling

Yiling and her maid, Lin, escaped from the burning house, fleeing to the bamboo forest. The maid had managed to grab a silk quilt on which they slept for a few hours. They awoke hungry. The maid told Yiling to wait while she ventured out to look for food. She would try going back to the kitchen if the house still stood.

Yiling waited a long while but Lin did not return. Yiling decided to search for her. It did not take her long to catch sight of the familiar figure. There was her maid dead on the ground, violated and still warm. Shocked and dazed, Yiling wandered on. Then she heard a man's coarse laughter. A soldier appeared, caught her wrist and she fainted.

Before the soldier could tear off her clothes three armed men surrounded him. On orders from an older man they killed the soldier and carried Yiling to him. They were the trained bodyguards of Duke Wu, one of the immigrants from Beijing with his own small army. Duke Wu had caught sight of Yiling being targeted by the soldier. He had given orders for her rescue and had her taken back to his home.

The Duke could see by her headdress and clothes that this was no ordinary girl. Intrigued, the Duke watched as she was washed, still unconscious, by his housekeeper. He saw a lithe, slender figure and a pretty face, certainly an extremely attractive young woman. The Duke left instructions for the young lady to be given the best of care, the best of herbal medicines and the best of food. She was to be brought to him a week later.

Duke Wu was a military man of standing but wanted the quieter life that Jian'an offered. He had wealth and a large but unostentatious property near the border, one of those not targeted by the Hu army. Wu still had a soldier's build and fighting skills, although his wisdom and experience taught him to avoid trouble unless provoked. He emerged to check the damage only after quiet settled on Jian'an once more. Chance had brought him out at that hour, otherwise Yiling would have been dead.

By the fourth day Yiling was strong enough to move around and stepped out to enjoy the garden. Without her knowledge the Duke observed her. He liked what he saw, and felt a stirring in his loins, even though he knew he was old enough to be her father. It thrilled him to learn that his body was still alive. He had grown children with thriving careers in Beijing and thought women were a thing of the past.

Yiling was assigned a personal maid. She found Pipi honest and trustworthy, learning much from her, including that two residences razed to the ground had been Hoong's and hers. That there were no survivors from her household, while those who fought the Hu army at Tolui's had all been killed. The news pained her and she grieved for her father, but most of all for Hoong, for she would never see him again. Pipi emphasised that Yiling would have been dead had she not been rescued by Duke Wu. Yiling owed her life to the Duke, although she would have preferred death without Hoong!

For three days Yiling experienced intense anguish as she absorbed the fact that her loved ones were all gone. She did not fear death, but the notion that she was meant to live out a sad earthly life slowly dominated her thoughts. As she walked towards the Duke's study, since he had sent for her, she recalled maid Pipi's words that she owed the Duke her life. Arriving at the doorway, she stood looking at the back of a tall figure with broad shoulders. He turned to face her.

It was a strong, stern and lined face with good features. Duke Wu looked her father's age, thought Yiling. His face softened as he smiled at her. He spoke what was on his mind. Wu told her he would marry her and she would be the mistress of his household. His wife had died many years ago and his two concubines lived separately in Beijing. He had lived by himself for some years.

Yiling acknowledged his announcement with a sad smile and agreed. The Duke was her saviour. The love of her life, Hoong, was gone, but her memories of him would always stay locked in her heart. She had no one and no home. Wu would protect and look after her. Two weeks after the sacking of Jian'an, Yiling married the Duke in a quiet ceremony.

Yiling was given a beautiful two-piece red bridal gown with a matching red veil. Her headdress was no less beautiful. It was what she would have wanted for her wedding, with the exception of the groom. The Duke's eldest son and two of his oldest friends came from Beijing for the ceremony. They could only gasp at the beauty and youth of the bride. The groom still had his good looks and wore a contented, satisfied look.

Yiling went through the ceremony willingly. She submitted herself to her husband. He was a gentle and loving husband. She had already decided to give him her loyalty and to be a good wife. But her love lay elsewhere, with someone who was gone from the earthly life.

Duke Wu the Military General

Duke Wu came from a family of wealth and prestige. His family could be traced back to the Tang dynasty, an outstanding period in Chinese history known for its peace, wealth and the flourishing of the arts. Wu inherited two items from this period. One was a white jade Ferghana horse the size of his hand. It was smooth and cool to the touch.

The other was a painting of Tang court ladies. The details of their robes were clearly painted in an array of Tang colours, looking so much like Japanese traditional costumes. In actual fact, the fashion had travelled to Japan from China with Buddhist scripts at the time. The Japanese had remained faithful to the fashion.

Wu was a third son. His two older brothers were top scholars destined for the bureaucracy and, hopefully, the prime ministership. There was a fourth son upon whom their parents doted. Unlike his brothers, Wu was not interested in books. He had a more athletic build, preferred an outdoor life and drifted to the military. His family's standing got him a position as a captain, but his own ability enabled him to rise up the ladder of success. China had so many borders to protect, so many wars to fight, a fearless young man with initiative would, with time and experience, became a general. It was no surprise that Wu received a dukedom when he retired.

Wu enjoyed his freedom as a young man. He lived life fast and sowed his wild oats. His fondness for drink and the ability to manage it endeared him to his soldiers. He was no alcoholic, for he had brains and control. He was popular with males and females. He had good enough looks, a roguish smile and charm to win many a female. Even at war he managed to have female company.

Wu also had filial piety, returning home to marry a girl chosen by his parents. She was from a family of wealth and standing, giving his parents further prestige. Well-to-do families customarily married their own kind. Wu's bride was both attractive and accomplished. She had been privately tutored. She could paint and embroider besides having studied the classics. However, she was far too serious and not a good conversationalist. In short, she was a bore!

The young lady had repeatedly been taught her duties as a good female while growing up. Firstly, she was to remain virtuous. Upon marriage she was to be a good wife and produce many sons. Her mother prayed continuously to goddess Kwan Yin that her only daughter be fertile, for infertility meant she would lose her place to other women. Together with this fact she was reminded that it was a man's world, and women were there to serve them. Coupling was for a man's pleasure and reproduction. She was the ideal vessel for such teachings, the perfect daughter.

Wu's wife gave him many sons but preferred the company of her children to that of her husband. She made no objections when he took a concubine. Then he took another, an even younger concubine. This time he seemed to have met his match, for she was bold enough to invade his privacy, venturing into his study to find him. Yet she fascinated him, for she had voluptuous lips, a large bust and an interest in his body, something seldom shown by "proper ladies". This concubine gave him one son and no more. She was not interested in childbearing and losing her shapely figure. She had learnt about contraceptive herbs, took them regularly, and they worked. After a while, Wu lost interest. She had little education, no lively mind, nothing except her body.

Wu was experienced in many ways. Years before, when he was posted to Beijing for military duty, he had rapidly become familiar with the big city, including the top courtesan establishments. These were no cheap whore houses but luxurious places with comfortable, tastefully furnished private rooms and first class food. The patrons were from rich and powerful families. The sons of the wealthy were the most popular customers. It was not unknown for a father and son to bump into each other. Even members of the royal family were guests and there had been rumours of visits by the Emperor!

The courtesans were carefully selected. Girls with outstanding good looks from poor families were bought by these places. The madams trained them into genteel young ladies. Many could play at least one instrument. They were trained to sing or even to paint. The expensive establishments offered young ladies with at least some education and the ability to converse with men. They had more to offer than just bodies.

The House of the Singing Orioles boasted of not having a single dissatisfied customer. The House of Peonies claimed they had the most beautiful girls, while the House of Magnolias professed to have the most beautiful voices.

Yiling the Wife

A week passed after the wedding before the Duke came to claim Yiling again. She was grateful that he gave her privacy and time to rest. Time to absorb that she had a new life, a husband, new responsibilities. Wu was also wise enough to realise that his bride was young, that she had accepted him and that he should not make too many demands on her. He had enough to keep himself busy already, being a wealthy man with property in Beijing, educated, and with interesting pastimes such as hunting and art.

On their wedding night when Wu made love to her, he found that, although apparently not a virgin, Yiling felt some pain and was far from being an experienced lover. He was convinced that she must have been raped by a soldier during the sacking of Jian'an. He would use all his expertise to remove her fear of men and draw her out! This second time he thought there was a moment of response from her body, which delighted him. Yiling had for the barest moment thought she was with Hoong, only to realise she was not and froze. She could not give herself freely to Wu, nor could she reject him. For the Duke, willing submission was enough and he could not ask for more. She did give him pleasure!

Yiling intrigued the Duke like none of the other women he knew. She had sad eyes and a faraway look. She had a quick mind, could hold a conversation and was a good listener. The Duke mused to himself that he would not die of boredom in his old age with her.

Wu was no fool. He had information brought to him of Yiling's background. He received news even of the lives of Shan and XiXi. He learnt of Shan's devotion to his wife and child and of the last few years when Shan had given himself up to drink and women. The Duke knew it must have been painful for Yiling.

Nothing was omitted. Shan, XiXi and Yiling kept to themselves and were happy that way! When Yiling reached the marriageable age of thirteen she had no suitor nor was she betrothed to anyone. She was not exposed to male company. She was a proper girl, unlikely to have liaisons, as she rarely went out. Only Yiling's maid and Batir knew of Hoong and Yiling' meetings in the bamboo forest. The maid was dead and Batir would never betray Hoong. Besides, it had been an innocent friendship until the last evening. Even Shan's uncle, who was always spying on them, knew nothing of importance.

Teck had come forward to claim Shan's vast properties as the last remaining relative, only later learning that Yiling had survived and married the Duke. Knowing Duke Wu was powerful and that he would not be able to get away with all the wealth, Teck went to the Duke to offer half of it to Yiling, saying that Shan had wanted the wealth to stay in the Gu family. Wu consulted Yiling, who was happy with the proposition, insisting that the matter was to go no further. She now had her own fortune and Wu had his. There was more than enough. The fortune later benefitted Yiling's two charities: saving young girls from being crippled through foot binding and rescuing abandoned wives and destitute widows.

The weeks passed after the wedding. Yiling started to throw up but she hid that from the Duke. Soon Wu noticed that her waistline was slowly disappearing. One morning he found her looking pale and unwell. He immediately sent for the family physician. She was indeed pregnant.

The shrewd Duke worked out that the conception of the child was very near their wedding. The child could be his. Otherwise, it must be due to the rape he thought that Yiling suffered when the sacking of Jian'an took place. Wu had never questioned her and she never spoke or ever referred to that unhappy time. Who knows? Wu decided that he would bring the child up as his own and love it as much as he loved his wife.

Some eight and a half months after the wedding a healthy, fair-skinned chubby boy child was born. There was much rejoicing.

The baby was named Bao, meaning precious, the name chosen by Yiling. The new mother spent many hours studying her child. The boy had a high nose and a wide jaw. Yiling's joy grew as she became convinced he was Hoong's child. Meanwhile it pleased the Duke to see Yiling's face become rounder as she put on some weight. Wu thought the baby's high nose looked like his. He remembered that his maternal grandfather had a square jaw. So the child must be his!

13

Hoong Survives

Fate had dealt Hoong a cruel blow but Fortune had not deserted him. The Emperor appointed a general to remedy the situation in both the state of Hu and in Jian'an, for the security of the empire was involved. Firstly, the Governor of Hu had to be completely crushed: killed or sent in chains to Beijing and publicly executed, the Hu army punished and a new army formed. Secondly, Jian'an had to be restored and protected by a new larger army.

General Wan was part of the new imperial army at Beijing. He was selected as there had been a recent reassessment of the Ming dynasty's military power. He worked closely with the Minister of Defence and Warfare and was feared by the Prime Minister and his cohorts. The Emperor Yongle was known to favour the military, as he had led many skirmishes against the tribes as a prince. News had also reached the Emperor that the Jurchen tribes in the north east were active and on the move. In the past the Hu state army had kept an eye on them.

Under Emperor Yongle the Ming dynasty was strong. Meritocracy was back. Whenever this happened the country prospered, for the bureaucracy functioned smoothly and there was justice. General Wan was one such example of ability and honesty. He had risen through the ranks through hard work and high principles. Corruption and sinecures irked him. Wherever Wan went he was on the lookout for talent and honesty. In his work to reorganise Hu he came across Hoong.

The first three months in Hu'xinzhou had been somewhat hazy to Hoong as he recovered his strength after the castration. But his ears pricked up when he heard that there was a badly wounded Mongol prisoner from Jian'an. Could it be Batir? The prisoner was said to be darker, smaller and more Mongol-looking than Hoong. That item of news got Hoong on his feet and off he went, checking the bunks where the wounded lay. When he made out the dark unshaven face of Batir he could not stop his silent tears and exclaimed aloud. Batir opened his eyes at the sound of Hoong's voice. Tears also flew fast and furious from the still-wounded Batir. From that moment they could not be separated. Hoong nursed Batir, feeding and cleaning him.

The strong, unusually good-looking young man caught Wan's eye. He sent his spies to bring all the information they could find on Hoong. Wan had watched him go through the military manoeuvres. Hoong was an excellent horseman. He could use the bow and arrow while riding. He could handle the long sword. Unbelievable! Someone must have trained him. That man must be an expert himself. To top it all Hoong was educated too. Was this possible?

Then the story of Tolui unfolded. General Wan was handed the file on Tolui.

The General learnt that Hoong was three when his grandfather took over his training, starting with horse riding. Hoong had taken to horses from the start. When given his first pony, Hoong had whispered into her large ears that he loved her and would marry her. He would not get off, falling asleep and having to be peeled off her back. Were his skills a gift from his Mongolian genes? General Wan learnt that Mongol children as young as two were strapped to the livestock and learnt the movement of animals at that age. From the time they were three they rode horses with a member of the family. It pleased the General that Tolui had married a Han lady, the daughter of the Han commander of the fortress of Jian'an. That their son had married another Han female, a scholar's daughter. No wonder Hoong did not have the hard look of the Mongols. The General thought Hoong looked more Han, although taller and tougher. Hah! He had enough Chinese blood. The General could see the intelligence in Hoong's eyes, although tinged with sadness. He understood when he learnt of Hoong's castration.

Coming across Hoong was a rare opportunity. Such a talented person was one he could train and keep at his side. He interviewed Hoong and asked if he would serve him.

Hoong felt he had nothing to lose but had one request, asking that Batir be allowed to come with him, for Batir was his kin and the only person left that he loved. This was granted unquestioningly, as the General had already decided to take on Batir as well, even though not as talented as Hoong.

Hoong and Batir trained in the new army while the General busily cleaned up Hu. He rooted out possible dissidents while keeping an eye on the tribes on the north-eastern Steppes. The General could see that Batir was no less a horseman than Hoong. The difference was that Batir was a faithful follower of Hoong's and had no ambition to lead. Hoong showed leadership but a greater interest in battle strategy.

Nearly nine months after Hoong's arrival in Hu'xinzhou, he and Batir prepared for their first battle.

On the morning of their encounter with the Jurchen tribes, Hoong woke before dawn with an unusual feeling of elation. He could not find a reason for the sudden overwhelming happiness, so he accepted it as a good omen for the battle about to take place. At precisely the same moment, somewhere in Jian'an, a newborn boy gave a lusty cry.

Hoong and Batir were glad that they faced the Jurchens and not the Mongols. Filled with excitement and fear, they both showed courage and fought well. Wily General Wan already knew that the gathering Jurchen tribes were no match for his Ming troops, but wanted the two young men tested. He kept his elite troops on standby, just in case. They were not needed.

The next attack came six months later, suddenly, and with twice the manpower. Hoong watched the battle formations, picking out the leaders and changes in manoeuvres. He learnt that the tribes preferred to remain independent, trusting only their own leaders. They were often suspicious of, and hostile to, other tribesmen. On their own they would never be strong enough. The danger lay in the chance that a charismatic, unusually strong leader could gain the allegiance of the hundreds of tribes, one like Genghis Khan.

Batir sallied forth to meet the Jurchens, leading a newly-trained detachment of warriors. He had not expected the large number of fighters in black that came pouring over the hills in the dawning light. Batir suddenly found himself isolated as Jurchen swordsmen swirled around him. He looked into the cold eyes of a tribesman who slowly raised his arm, poised with a sword to cut him down. Nevertheless, he would die fighting. Then it happened! The sword dropped to the ground as an arrow pierced the chest of the warrior.

The arrow came from Hoong, who was leading a squad of archers on horseback. Hoong's great courage in saving Batir was an example to the Ming troops and encouraged them to surge forward as well.

Following behind was General Wan with his Ming Cavalry. That ended the battle. The Jurchens turned and fled back towards the Steppes. Victory was sweet!

Hoong found the military superior of his dreams in General Wan. Many changes took place before that second battle with the Jurchens. First was the arrival of horses from Beijing, followed by armour, bows and arrows with the latest metal arrowheads, swords and lances. The soldiers were drunk with joy for days. General Wan's patron, the Minister of War and Defence, had secured a bonus for supplies in the Court at Beijing.

Hoong was also gifted a fine horse by the General. His joy was great, for it was a Ferghana horse! As grandfather Tolui told him, when you find the right horse, you will move as one. The generous supply of horses meant Hoong had his squad of mobile archers. From the smiles and hilarity within the Hu'xinzhou fortress, the uninitiated would get the impression that the military was a happy place to work. That evening, after the second battle, amid the laughter and tuneless singing of the soldiers, Hoong was ordered to see the General in his room the next morning.

Hoong entered the spacious, comfortable yet simple room he had been in twice before. The General was not there, but in the middle of his large wooden desk lay a book. Hoong went closer to look. *The Art of War* by Sun Tze. Hoong was intrigued and started to read. "Know your enemy, know his weaknesses and strengths. Likewise know your own." Absolutely right, thought Hoong. Hoong's memory travelled into Tolui's study. Had he seen such a tome on the shelves?

His thoughts were interrupted by the clearing of a throat behind him. It was the General.

'So you are interested in battle strategy. You were so engrossed you did not hear me coming in. We shall discuss battle strategy this evening when you come to have dinner with me. For the time being I just want to congratulate you for the courage and skill shown during the battle.'

General Wan handed the book to Hoong, saying it was a gift, to read it and return with his ideas that evening. He had another copy in his library in his home in Beijing, so he could spare this one.

Hoong returned to be treated to a simple yet delicious meal with the General. It was rumoured that the General had brought one of his cooks from Beijing. There were just three dishes. Firstly a filleted chicken cooked in wine, thus known as drunken chicken. Next, a thick black mushroom cooked in an oyster sauce, and lastly a slightly spicy nut dish cooked with bamboo shoots. It had been a long time since Hoong had such tasty food. The General's cook, when asked about his secrets, would always reply 'It is a very hot wok and tasty sauces!'

Hoong told General Wan he was very aware that the Ming Cavalry was among the best around. The troops were well-trained, disciplined and capable of numerous battle formations. They were able to fight in different and difficult terrains, they were not only physically tough but mentally as well. But one thing the Chinese troops did not possess was the ability of the tribes to shoot from horseback. The other factor was the ferocity of the tribesmen, who showed no fear of death. This was true of the thousands of horsemen led by Genghis Khan.

Hoong had other observations to add.

In Hoong's view, the phenomenon of Genghis Khan was a once in a lifetime event. His own two battles with the Jurchens revealed that the tribes were suspicious by nature, unwilling to be directed by those they hardly knew. In his first battle he remembered the calls of the young tribesmen to their leader, Anu. They had rallied to Anu but the Ming army was too strong for them.

In the second battle the numbers had doubled but they fought as two armies, not one. Anu was there with his warriors. When the Ming troops charged it was the other group that turned and ran. Anu and his followers called but the other group did not respond. Overwhelmed, Anu's forces had no choice but to flee as well.

Hoong wanted his armed horsemen to be as good as, if not better than, the tribesmen. His special warriors would be the "surprise element" and, with further improved formations, they would be a boon to any Ming army.

The meeting ended with a bemused smile on General Wan's face. This was the son-in-law he wanted for his beautiful daughter, father for his grandchildren. Unfortunately, it was not to be, for despite his strength and stature, Hoong was a eunuch. But Hoong's secret would be safe with him.

14

Hoong Learns the Strategies of War

And so the rest of the year passed.

Hoong threw himself into his work in Hu'xinzhou. It was several months after the second battle when a group of fifty young men assembled in front of the fortress, calling for warrior Hoong. General Wan soon found out what the excitement was about. The spokesman of the group informed him that they wanted to train as fighters under Hoong. They were not "totally useless", the spokesman explained, as they could ride and had some experience at handling swords and fighting. The keen eyes of the General could see that some looked fully Mongol, while others were Mongol and Han mixed. They were from both Jian'an and Hu.

Hmmm … they were worth considering. They were steps ahead of raw recruits and could be controlled if they were loyal to a leader they had already identified. Hoong was sent for with haste. On arrival, he sized up the situation. Hoong assessed the group. They did not appear to be an unruly mob, but earnest young men.

He nodded to the General, he was willing to train them. They would be the second group of his Flying Horsemen. It was a happy Hoong who trained the new men at dawn each morning, while in the late morning he went through the exercises with his first group of Flying Horsemen. Always at his side was a very fit, fully bearded Batir.

Meanwhile, General Wan was busy preparing two reports, one for the Emperor, the other for the Minister of War and Defence.

Batir and Hoong were out and about every day. They would take their horses at dawn to hone their riding skills and practise mobile archery. As children they had learnt from grandfather Tolui to guide their horses just by gripping with their thighs, meaning their arms were free for using the bow and arrow. Their expertise with horses meant they could concentrate on their swords and their enemy. The morning rides enabled them to practise swivelling their bodies on horseback. It was easier for Batir, as he was smaller. For Hoong, who was taller and larger than average, the practise was vital while he was still a teenager. True, riding out of the fortress was not without its dangers, but at the same time they learnt awareness, a keen eye for movements around them and a good ear for the slightest sounds. And the scouts who kept an eye on the tribes also ensured the safety of the two young men.

They bonded even further. A keen swimmer, Batir taught Hoong all he knew about moving safely through water. Batir found the streams and waterfalls where they cleansed and refreshed themselves. Hoong took every opportunity to wash. The men always wore their three quarter length inner pants, so Hoong's secret was safe even if he bathed with his soldiers.

Hoong additionally mastered much about the non-combat aspects of warfare during his four and a half years at the Hu'xinzhou fortress. Firstly about the messengers, then the scouts, and finally the spies. A messenger's job was straightforward: deliver the message. No more than that. A scout was required to provide more information with regard to enemy numbers and terrain. Finally, a spy would infiltrate the enemy and risk a terrible death. For this last group, the risks were considered worthwhile if payment was large. For a young spy, the knowledge that his siblings and parents would keep a roof over their heads and food on the table made it worthwhile sacrificing his life. Yet his information could mean saving the lives of many soldiers Hoong never begrudged paying the scouts and spies well.

Hoong and Batir found out something important one evening: there was an aborted gathering of tribes!

A young scout they had befriended took them out through the nearby hills. Quietly, they reach a high point overlooking the valley below. Camped there were three separate Jurchen groups. They watched, hardly breathing! After a short time the tribesmen stirred and several men in grand robes appeared. There was argument and fierce shouting. The men strode back towards their respective camps, each group swiftly breaking down their gers, gathering their meagre possessions and moving in different directions. At that point the scout signalled to Hoong and Batir to ride back to the fortress as fast as they could.

When they returned, the three young men found General Wan and the scout gave his interpretation of what had happened. The appearance of three distinct groups of gers revealed three different tribes of Jurchens. That they stayed separate showed a lack of unity. The shouting between the leaders meant there was disagreement and that they had decided not to join in battle. General Wan added that, besides the lack of trust, the Jurchen tribes probably knew the Ming troops at the fortress were too strong for them, although he also noted that the enemy should never be underestimated.

Hoong thus grasped a weakness of the Jurchens. They might be ferocious fighters but were also fiercely independent and distrusting, even of their own kind. Sun Tzu's words echoed in Hoong's mind. "Know your enemy, their strengths and weaknesses."

Hoong learnt much on his own and under the guidance of General Wan. He worked with the stationary archers at the fortress. As the presence of the tribes slowly diminished, Hoong and Batir had time to devise various strategies. The archers were lined up along the wall and ordered to shoot as far as they could. Hoong and Batir measured the distances the archers could reach with the latest equipment. The range and size of the bows and what damage the arrowheads could cause. They worked on the smaller bows that could still be lethal from horseback. Archery had been part of war from the earliest of days in Chinese history, not the monopoly of the barbarian tribes. Defence archery at the fortresses was a vital component of warfare, while the cavalry waited for the right time to burst through the fortress gates. Hoong learnt to lead as a mobile archer as well as to lead the cavalry to war. By the end of that year he was no mean military leader!

Back in the residence of Duke Wu, a young mother full of laughter played with her infant son. An older man watched them. It was a happy scene.

Months passed. Imperial orders reached Hu'xinzhou. General Wan was recalled to Beijing. There had been peace since the second battle. The Jurchens seemed to have moved on. Tribal gatherings were few. Even at the Great Wall outside Beijing there were no harassing tribes. Jian'an was thriving again, and its reinforced fortress functioned well. Communications with Hu were exchanged every day. The strong army at Hu kept a watchful eye on Jian'an. It was time for Wan the General to return to Beijing where he would be of greater use.

Wan the statesman also thought deeply about Hoong's future. Hoong's country had need of his talents, but he was too young to be left in charge of Hu, having not even reached the age of twenty. Wan had a very capable and experienced assistant to leave behind as a commander. Hoong was to follow the General to Beijing. He would be useful to the war faction, to the General and the minister, in the court politics at Beijing. Hoong was important enough to have Batir as an assistant and his first group of Flying Horsemen as his personal guards.

Wan relayed his plans to Hoong, who agreed. The General would leave for Beijing and Hoong would follow with Batir and his personal guards two weeks later.

The second squadron of Flying Horsemen had to be left behind at Hu'xinzhou, as advised by General Wan. Although disappointed,

Hoong's last words to them were to continue with their exercises and manoeuvres, for who knew when they would be called to join him?

Batir planned their journey to Beijing. He felt that Hoong would be leaving that part of the world forever. Although Hoong spoke little of his past, Batir knew that Hoong would like to say goodbye to Jian'an, as he himself did. Batir's route through Jian'an passed the empty site of Tolui's property. Although the residence was no more the neighbourhood was still the same.

That morning, Batir rode out just ahead of Hoong.

On the same day, Yiling decided to go into the centre of Jian'an. Just before the market stalls were the fresh fruit stalls. Little Bao had discovered peaches. Strange that mother XiXi, she, and now Bao loved peaches. With her maid, Yiling made her way to the stalls.

Batir had ridden ahead to clear the streets and warn that a victory parade was on its way. The two women rushed to opposite sides of the street. Yiling did not recognise Batir, but Batir caught sight of her before she hid behind the tables at the noodle stall. Batir was shocked to see Yiling, having thought her dead these last few years!

Next came the blare of trumpets announcing the Commander and armed warriors on horseback. Yiling had good eyesight. What she saw made her almost collapse with disbelief. Her heart pounded. It was a stern-faced Hoong, looking much older, more mature, with wider shoulders, for it was now almost three years since that night.

That he did not search for her meant he thought she had been killed. Yilin's face twisted with sorrow and her eyes filled with tears. She would love Hoong forever but they were not meant for each other. She knew it was better for Hoong to go on to a greater future. Besides, she had just learnt that she was pregnant to the Duke. Was it to Beijing Hoong was going? His armour showed he was of rank and he led the troops. Yiling was glad that her maid was at the other side of the road and not a witness to her agony.

Batir was still in shock, but had one of his men follow Yiling to find out what he could about her. He continued his journey. He watched Hoong's sad smile as they passed where grandfather Tolui's residence had been. Hoong had learnt early that life could be brutal and one had no control over events

Batir's journey to Beijing was one of doubt and worry. By the time they reached Beijing, Batir had decided he would not tell Hoong that Yiling was alive and had seen her with his own eyes. His spy had reported that Yiling had been rescued by a certain Duke Wu after the sacking of Jian'an. The Duke, elderly compared to them, was a wealthy and powerful military person and that she had a child by him. Informing Hoong that she lived might result in rash action. Batir knew that Hoong loved Yiling deeply. And now Hoong was a eunuch, what future was there for them? Better to let him believe she was dead, although she had seen him and knew he lived. She had a new life, was somebody's wife, and the mother of somebody's child.

He shook his head sadly.

Batir

Perhaps life was not totally cruel, for Hoong had Batir. Batir was Hoong's guardian angel. But there was much to Batir that Hoong did not know.

Batir was a bit of a wild man. Early in life he was aware of the attraction of females. He had found them and enjoyed them. It was he who introduced women to Hoong. After joining the fortress at Hu'xinzhou, while Hoong never took leave, Batir spent all his off-duty days in the city. He knew many women and had finally found himself a delicate-looking Chinese woman as a partner. He would never tell Hoong of his activities for fear of hurting him.

Hoong would forever come before anyone else for Batir. It was a sick Hoong who dragged himself around to nurse a badly injured Batir. It was Hoong who shot the tribesman who would have killed him. His promotion in the army was also due to Hoong. Through into the mists of the past, he recalled the fair-skinned, chubby toddler with the sturdy little legs chasing after him. 'Ba ... Ba ... please do not leave little Hoong'. As the child grew, he would bring food hidden in his clothes for Batir. He would share whatever he had with Batir. These recollections were some of Batir's most beautiful memories.

Hoong was also responsible for Batir's trust in the Chinese and willingness to serve them, as the Mongol families of Batir and Tolui had received kindness from them. Because of Hoong.

Batir had his talents too. He was a dedicated fighter and a willing worker. He tried to bring out the best in the recruits he trained and to inspire them. Batir helped Hoong train his two groups of Flying Horsemen. All the non-Han soldiers flocked to Batir and flourished under him. He was the officer to see when Hoong was not available or when they just wanted someone to sound out.

Batir was also responsible for many light moments in Hu'xinzhou.

One day identical twin brothers appeared at the fortress. They asked for Batir, saying they had just turned sixteen and were ready for their first jobs. They claimed to be multi-talented. They could cook, wash and entertain, for they could sing and dance, but were not trained as fighters.

It transpired that the twins were nephews of Batir's Chinese partner, although their mother was Mongol. Physically they looked completely Chinese but were of small build. At least Batir could vouch that they came from a good family. Hoong had to be consulted before the twins could be accepted as new recruits. General Wan had complete faith in Hoong's judgment, giving him the power to recruit. Hoong appeared and the entertainment started.

First the boys danced acrobatically, leaping and kicking. They showed off their strong limbs, bringing whistles and applause from the soldiers. Hoong recalled his poorer performance before Yiling at the bamboo forest years ago. Then the boys did a duet. They sang as a pair of lovers and the "female" sang exceptionally well. The male's attempts at kissing and groping the "female" caused hooting and cat calls. The general feeling of the audience was that the twins would bring much laughter to the fortress. Hoong's verdict was to put them on hold. He wanted to know whether they were any good as soldiers.

The next day the twins were tested on horse riding and archery. Was it their Mongolian genes or had they been tipped off and already practised? The announcement came on the third morning that they were accepted. Many of the men went up to Batir to congratulate him.

The twins were named Lu and Lui. Many a time they asked their mother why they could not have different faces like every other child. In time they learnt there were many advantages in being a twin. They had often pretended to be the other when faced with punishment for their pranks. They were never shy. There was always so much fun when they made fools of their friends. As new recruits the two of them would fight one man, leaving him confused and exhausted, not realising the first twin had disappeared and it was a fresh second twin in his place. In the house of pleasure in Hu'xinzhou, the House of Snow Blossoms, they had paid expensively for a private room and exchanged places late at night, leaving the lady amazed at the young man's energy!

Both Hoong and Batir quickly noticed that the younger twin had a mole on his neck, missing from the other twin. They were never fooled, but pretended not to know who was who. While others looked the twins straight in the face, the cousins looked straight for the mole.

They were wholesome boys, for they came from a loving family. Their father, a merchant, was often away from home, but their mother made up for everything. This large Mongol woman was full of love and laughter. Lu and Lui left behind ten year old twin sisters for their mother to cuddle and love.

A year later, in place of the two mischievous boys were two serious youths much loved by Hoong and Batir. They became part of the group following the young leaders to Beijing.

15

Beijing: Corridors of Power

General Wan spent much of the fortnight before he returned to Beijing in serious conversation with Hoong.

The General was a man of deep convictions, a patriot who would give his life for his country. He was also a student of the history of China. So many Chinese patriots died tragic deaths back in the mists of time, such as the poet Qu Yuan some eighteen centuries earlier during the time of the Warring States. Qu drowned himself when the ruler rejected his ministerial advice. From his death arose the festival of Zongzi, when the rice bundle delicacy was eaten. The traditional Dragon Boat Festival was also associated with Zongzi.

It was during one of his conversations with Hoong that Wan learnt they shared the same military hero, General Yue Fei of the twelfth century Southern Song dynasty. And of course, they both revered the military strategist, Sung Tze, whose fifteen hundred year old lessons on warfare applied even to the modern day.

As for Yue Fei, he was lauded in history and literature. Hoong heard the legend from his mother when he was only six. Yue Fei was known for his military skill, courage and humanitarian beliefs. He cared for his soldiers on and off the field, but also for the civilians, peasants and simple villagers. His love for others was demonstrated by the story of him as a young man faced with a dilemma. He wanted to save his country from the Jurchens, but as an only son he could not leave his elderly mother, for he owed her filial piety, compelling him to stay and care for her. No amount of persuasion could make him leave. She finally resolved the problem when she made him take off his shirt and tattooed four Chinese characters on his back: Jing Zhong Bao Guo, meaning serve the country loyally. He never lost a battle, even when outnumbered. Unfortunately, Yue Fei was sentenced to death at the age of 39 as a result of treachery.

Wan shook his head sadly. Luckily this was fifteenth century Ming China and things had changed – hopefully. Hoong was too talented to be left in Hu. But would he be able to escape the malice and evil that lingered in the imperial court? A fine web of intrigue had grown over the decades and death seemed to lurk in every corner of the imperial palace. It could even be seen in the new palace, which was to become known as the Forbidden City.

The use of eunuchs to guard and serve the Emperor's harem had originally been considered the work of a genius. It ensured that no bastard, no son of a lowly worker, could inherit the imperial throne through subterfuge. However, the number and power of the eunuchs had gone unchecked. The number of concubines had also multiplied, so too the tally of imperial offspring. Many ladies of the harem never even met the Emperor, yet no one sought to curtail their recruitment. Perhaps because many were political unions. The harem could only be a hotbed of intrigue as ambitious females and eunuchs formed their own private alliances.

General Wan wondered how a country could function with so much distraction at the seat of power. Too much depended on having a strong and able leader. There were many factions at court. Uncles, brothers, and cousins competed for the Emperor's ear, while eunuchs and concubines combined forces to influence him. The bureaucracy and the military competed for funds. The corrupt and ambitious had their own agendas.

The General felt sorry for the current young Emperor. Who does he trust, who can he turn to? Hoong was someone who could help to give the Ming dynasty strength, stability and peace. The General felt he had to do his best to help Hoong achieve this.

General Wan warned Hoong that Beijing and the Emperor were dangerous, that the job of serving the country and Emperor was often thankless, with death hovering around the corner. He could see the sincerity and conviction on Hoong's face. Wan had never before met anyone like him, and the thought that Hoong would never succumb to the wiles or temptations of a woman left him with a wry smile on his face.

Wan had already prepared an area on the city outskirts as quarters for Hoong's personal guards. Armed troops were not permitted entry into the city, only the elite imperial guards, who were quartered at a far corner of the Forbidden City. If summoned, these guards could storm into the palace in moments.

When Hoong reached Beijing the first squadron of the Flying Horsemen were with him, so too the twins and, of course, Batir. These three followed Hoong everywhere. The General was there to meet them and directed the Flying Horsemen to their quarters.

Wan took Hoong and the small team to his large home, where he had guest accommodation.

Keen for the Emperor to receive fresh advice, the General and the Minister of War and Defence had worked hard to arrange a private audience with him. The new fleet was the Emperor's passion. With the flurry of activity and spending on the massive sea vessels and the impressive presence of Admiral Zheng He, they feared the military would be forgotten. China was gaining so much prestige with Zheng's voyages to south east Asia and even Africa. The Emperor needed to be reminded that land power came first. The General was convinced that Hoong would impress the Emperor.

At the appointed time, Hoong and his superiors proceeded to one of the many audience halls in the Forbidden City. To their surprise, they encountered the Prime Minister and his closest followers, who appeared to be heading in the same direction. Smiling, the Prime Minister greeted the Minister of War and Defence, saying he had heard about the audience and gained permission from the Emperor to attend. Spies! This was Beijing, where secrets rarely remain as such.

Hoong was an eloquent speaker and impressive figure, but the presence of a hostile group destroyed any chance of the intimacy and frankness intended. The Prime Minister had his legitimate concerns. The building of the mighty fleet, a feat previously unknown, not only to China, but to the rest of the world, would doubtlessly mean there would have to be economies in many other areas. The bureaucracy had its own plans and projects for spending the national revenue. The bureaucracy also nursed a hatred of eunuchs and Admiral Zheng He was a eunuch. No matter how great his exploits, the bureaucracy would ignore him and scholars would never write about him.

Bad luck for the Minister and the General, Hoong was now known to the Prime Minister and his cohorts, plus others who had seen him at the Forbidden City that morning. Let him learn that Beijing was no playground for a young ambitious military man.

Treachery at the Royal Hunt

Life at the Imperial Court was a constant battle, even when the country appeared to be enjoying peace. The military faction had to be cautious. At that point in time, the only position General Wan could find for Hoong was that of bodyguard to Prince Yen. To appoint Hoong as commander of an army, even to a border area, would arouse the ire and suspicion of the Prime Minister and his power bloc.

Prince Yen was the most promising of the Emperor's numerous sons, but he was the child of a concubine. The Emperor had already named his heir: the eldest and legal son of the Empress. A tall serious-looking scholarly person with a poor physical build, he had already married the Prime Minister's daughter. The Prince had even given the Emperor a grandchild. The Prime Minister was keen to protect his son-in-law against potential threats, including other imperial sons and ambitious uncles.

There was much excitement at Court, as the annual royal hunt was fast approaching. Here was an opportunity for princes and their cousins to exhibit themselves to the Emperor, highlight their physical and intellectual skills, and prove they had the attributes to qualify for the throne if the opportunity arose. Each competitor was allowed a companion, often a trusted bodyguard or friend. The quest was to shoot as many animals as possible. Animals had to be killed by the competitor's personal arrows, loosed only by the competitor himself. Cheating would cause shame and outrage. The more dangerous the animal, the greater number of points. There would later be a banquet in Beijing to honour the champion, who would be allowed to sit next to the Emperor.

Batir was sent by the General to ensure that all was well. He was permitted no part in the hunt and could only lurk in the shadows.

Hoong found Prince Yen open and likeable. Young, spontaneous and eager, Prince Yen had much to learn, particularly about political life. They were the same age, but Hoong was more mature and rational, having had to learn fast to survive.

The drums sounded, the trumpets blared, the signal was given. The excited prince shot off, Hoong racing after him to keep pace. They came to the first crossroads.

Before them was a wide clear path, while to the left was a narrow, darker route. This way had more bushes and undergrowth, but was more promising for wild animals.

Hoong advised the Prince to take the more open route, but a voice called out 'Left, left, take the narrow left route.' Prince Yen thought it was the voice of one of his cousins. He veered left and cantered away. Hoong gave chase but the prince had disappeared. A short time later Hoong came across a riderless horse, the Prince's horse. The Prince was missing. Hoong was in trouble.

Hoong dismounted and went to examine the other horse, which was limping. Could it have tripped and thrown off the rider? Hoong scanned the area. Not far off he spied an unusually dark area with many small branches around it. Getting closer, Hoong found it was the opening of a deep pit. Hoong looked down. He called out, as it was too deep and dark to see whether there was anything at the bottom. There was a faint call in reply. Hoong had found the Prince!

Hoong returned to his horse and from the saddlebag brought out a long thick strong rope. Hoong never travelled without one.

He tied one end of the rope to a nearby tree and walked back to the pit with the other end. Tying the rope around his waist, he abseiled to the bottom, where an arm reached for him. The relieved Prince told Hoong he thought he was going to join his dead mother. He had been thrown when his horse shied as a hare darted under its hooves. He had struggled up only to fall into the pit after a few steps. Who would find him in such a desolate place!

With his injured arm the Prince could not climb the rope unaided. Hoong had Prince Yen climb on his back and clamp his legs around Hoong's waist like a horse, his good arm around Hoong's shoulder. Painstakingly, Hoong hauled the two of them out of the pit and onto his horse. Leading the Prince's horse behind them, the two young men made their way back to the grounds of the royal hunt.

As they reached the royal stands they saw a search party of soldiers with flares about to set out. The skies were darkening and the last competitor to return had been back for quite some time. Prince Yen's supporters had just learnt that he was missing and gratefully met Hoong and his passenger.

The Prince was taken back to the palace to recuperate. Hoong was surrounded by soldiers and held down in readiness for punishment, possibly even execution, for dereliction of duty. He should never have allowed the Prince out of his sight!

Again, it was faithful Batir to the rescue. He had waited anxiously for Hoong and Prince Yen to return and was beside himself with fear as daylight slowly faded. It was with great joy that he made out the two men on one horse leading a riderless horse. But the soldiers had fallen on Hoong the moment they had retrieved the Prince, too many to fight. Better to take the news to General Wan immediately. He would know what to do. Hoong would be safe in prison for the night.

The General went that night with the news to the Minister of War and Defence. The Minister would attend court the next day and try to save Hoong. Who could be behind the plot to kill Prince Yen? It was no mere accident! Was this an attempt to get rid of Hoong, too? Not surprising, this was Beijing!

At the Emperor's Court session the next day, a junior minister from the Prime Minister's camp called for Hoong to be executed, as a royal prince had been injured. The Minister of War and Defence stepped forward, begging that Hoong's life be spared. Hoong had brought the Prince home. He was not merely a competent warrior, but an excellent fighter. He had helped defeat the Jurchen tribes and reestablished order in Hu. As he finished there was a disturbance as Prince Yen appeared. The Prince appealed to his father, saying that Hoong was not a villain but his saviour. That he had been tricked into following the path leading to the trap.

Until the Prince's intervention the Emperor had thought of Hoong merely as another bright young spark new to Beijing. China had thousands of such men. What was one more? Perhaps he could be an example, held up as punishment and a show of the Emperor's power.

The Minister of War and Defence had foreseen such a possibility. He stepped forward again and begged the Emperor to consider his proposal. Since Hoong was a brilliant warrior and the kingdom was in need of such men, why not send him as a military officer to the Great Wall just outside Beijing to help with the defences and strengthening of the Wall.

A smile spread across the face of the Prime Minister. That was not a bad idea. His agreement would make him look magnanimous. Hoong would no longer be a threat in Beijing. Who knew? Hoong would probably languish and never leave the Wall, as happened to so many other political opponents!

So Hoong's next assignment was to the Great Wall. The Minister of War and Defence and General Wan still had enough power to arrange for Batir, the twins and the Flying Horsemen to be stationed there with Hoong.

16

Life Continues at Jian'an

Yiling returned to Duke Wu's residence with her emotions in turmoil after catching a glimpse of Hoong leading the Ming army through the streets of Jian'an. She rejoiced at learning that Hoong was alive, but grieved at the thought that they were destined to be apart. She was married and pregnant with somebody else's child. She passed the next few days in deep sorrow.

Fortunately, the Duke had just gone to Beijing for a fortnight. He would visit every few months, for he still had family and property there. Wu had a special relationship with his eldest son, Hua, with whom he would stay. There was love and respect between them.

Yiling gradually pulled herself together. She acknowledged that one has no choice but to accept what one is given in life. She had to be thankful for her son Bao. He was such a blessing, such a wonderful child, gentle, undemanding, always happy to see her as she was to see him. By the time Wu returned she was her pleasant, practical self.

The Duke was overjoyed to learn of her pregnancy. She had wanted to be absolutely sure before she told him. In fact, on his return from Beijing he had found her throwing up. He would not have gone away had he known. It boosted his pride to know that he could still father a child! To have a baby with Yiling was more than he had dreamed of! Wu always retained a seed of doubt about whether Bao could be his child, even though he had come to love the delightful child as his own.

As Yiling's stomach swelled so did the Duke's delight. Yiling's face developed a healthy glow and Wu looked younger, for his joy was great. But again fate stepped in. Even with all the caution in the world Yiling could not avoid a freak accident.

Yiling was almost eight months pregnant. Everything had seemed perfect. Then a swallow flew straight at her, striking her in the chest before falling to the ground. It happened so fast, Yiling tried to catch the falling bird, tripped and fell heavily on her stomach. It was a bad fall and she went into labour. A weeping Duke strictly instructed the physician to save the mother. He would not want to live without her. Indeed, Yiling lived but the perfectly formed boy child died.

During the next few months Wu experienced a sorrow he had not thought possible. He was told that Yiling would most likely survive, as she was young, but she would never have another child. Wu consoled himself that he still had her, for otherwise life would be meaningless. Many mornings passed with Wu and Bao sitting next to Yiling's bed, gazing at her pale visage. An old face and a small face looking down at Yiling with so much love, willing her to live.

Slowly, Yiling grew in strength. When she was fully recovered Hua brought his wife to visit. Hua appreciated Yiling. He could see her influence in the gentleness his father now displayed and how much Wu loved her. She was a far cry from the frivolous women with whom his father associated in his younger days. He recalled an old Chinese saying that a good woman brought out the best in men.

Hua also thought highly of his own wife, Mi Mi, who had given him two sons and a daughter. She was educated and accomplished, could paint and do beautiful embroidery. Hua thought that Mi Mi would be good company for Yiling, while his father could do with company too. He was right, and they stayed for two months.

Those months were a revelation to Yiling, for she came to understand how foot-bound women coped with life. Mi Mi was an example of the classical daughter, kind, gentle and helpful, exactly what Yiling needed during her recuperation. She taught Yiling the basics of painting and helped her discover that she had some talent for embroidery. Yes, Yiling even learnt to appreciate the dainty little feet that were always covered by exquisitely embroidered handmade shoes. But at what cost?

Mi Mi was surprised to find that Yiling had "big feet". The feet of all her relatives and acquaintances were bound. Only servants and peasant women had ugly, large feet.

It seemed that upper-class women had no problem with fertility. Their problem was mobility. Beautiful scenery had to be admired from afar, so too lakes, ponds, even flower gardens. Mi Mi had been taught to avoid uneven ground, narrow paths, pebbled paths, steep areas – even walking in her own gardens!

From Mi Mi, Yiling learnt that walking could be painful. Mi Mi went through the daily ritual of soaking her feet in hot water with the addition of a small handful of salt. Mi Mi's maid did this for her mistress each evening, massaging the deformed toes and drying them. Yiling saw the relief on Mi Mi's face when she retired to bed. Was the pain caused by the weight of the body on the feet, or was it pain from the broken bones and binding, or both?

Yiling was truly grateful for Mi Mi's friendship, gaining much from the visit, but two issues deeply perplexed her as a result.

The first was foot-binding. How could mothers allow their daughters to be crippled? Seeing the results up close reminded Yiling of her childhood encounter with Lady Ee. The other issue was the inequality between men and women. Why did Chinese women undermine their own kind by teaching them to be subservient to the men? There was much to ponder.

The Chinese Opera

There were many facets to Yiling's character, for she had inherited much from her parents, Shan and XiXi. It was from her mother that she developed a love for the Chinese Opera. In fact, XiXi had a cousin who became the star of the Anhui Hechun Troupe.

This cousin had visited a few times from Anhui and had even brought the troupe for a private performance. That was one of the rare occasions when they entertained the elite of Jian'an society. The privileged had their grand opera, which was not for the public, but in the poor villages there was also the opera at the annual festivities, which the peasants enjoyed no less.

XiXi learnt much from her cousin and it filtered down to Yiling. The performers were chosen as children, for the training took many years and was most rigorous. First the child had to be trained to sing, rigid opera-style, then to dance and do acrobatics while still young and supple. The acting came last.

The teacher, known as the Si Fu or Master, had complete control over the child. Punishment was common and use of the cane frequent. The Si Fu was like a god. The pupil did all the washing and cooking, and if it was not up to the Si Fu's standard then punishment was the result. The denial of food was not uncommon and many a pupil went to bed hungry.

The student had to learn perfect face painting. The audience knew when to clap or boo because the painting enabled them to recognise the hero, the villain and others. This was particularly important in the villages. The heavy painting took a toll on the performers' faces. Creams and massages faithfully followed each performance. Failure to follow the rules resulted in poor complexions and punishment for disobedience.

Opera existed since ancient times. It was written that traditional Chinese opera had been performed over a thousand years beforehand, during the Three Kingdoms Period. The Tang dynasty was a time when opera was vastly popular, with even royalty involved. Emperor Tai Zong was reputed to have written the famous opera "Liyan" (Pear Garden). Whenever culture flourished, as in Song dynasty times, opera flourished. The first opera that Yiling saw as a child was by the

Anhui Hechun Troupe, which specialised in military performances. Combat scenes were accompanied by drums, gongs, fluttering flags and fast music. Music for quiet scenes was produced by the pipa, flute and percussion instruments. The elaborate costumes, the painted faces and the array of battle instruments captivated the child. It was the troupes with the most sponsors or rich patrons that had the best costumes and background scenes.

Opera continued to flourish during the mid fifteenth century, the prosperous Ming dynasty days. It was not until 1790, when the four famous Anhui opera troupes combined, that it became known as the

Beijing Opera. The older, more gentle Kunqu Opera was known to have contributed much to the Beijing Opera.

Peasants, the uneducated, and even petty thieves gained some knowledge of China's literature and history through opera performances. Many a peasant woman lived for the village festivals when the opera was performed. Did they pass down their love for the opera with the milk from their bodies that they fed to their children?

And what stories were presented by the Opera? Sometimes a complete tale, but mostly it was sketches from famous Chinese folklore. It could be battle scenes featuring heroes from "The Romance of the Three Kingdoms." Another much loved story was "Water Margin". It told of outcasts who banded together to protect the common people and fight for justice. It is not difficult to understand how villagers venerated and loved these two stories. With the upper classes, the "Legend of General Yue Fei" was most popular. Yue Fei stood for loyalty and love for the country. Idealistic youth from well-to-do families with a military background idolised him.

Thus, opera was history and literature presented using music, song, dance, martial arts, acrobatics and costume artistry. In short, it was the complete package!

In contrast, the local storyteller was also owed a debt for adding to the villagers' knowledge of history. His eloquence and imagination while relating Chinese stories thrilled the young men who came to listen to him at the tea houses or local stalls. His reward was a humble copper coin.

17

The Child Bao and Yiling

'Mama, Mama, come help, a little girl is being beaten!'

Bao had left Yiling only moments before to investigate a noise as they walked through the poor part of Jian'an, made up of small wooden shacks. Bao was four years old and had begun accompanying Yiling on her fortnightly early morning shopping trips to the market.

Yiling rushed over. Indeed, there was a heavily pregnant woman with a raised cane pursuing a girl of five or six years. Of late Bao had started to refer to girls under the age of eight as little and himself as being older. Maybe it was a male thing, mused Yiling.

'Don't you dare run away from me! Stay still and receive your punishment!' Cowering just inside a doorway were two little boys around three years of age.

Yiling rushed forward. 'Madam, you are not in a position to strain yourself. You can induce labour. Think of your poor little children!'

Yiling took the cane away and helped the woman to a seat inside the shack where the boys stood. 'Here I am, willing to use my precious savings to get my daughter's feet bound so that the family can have a better future. The ungrateful wretch cries and protests she does not want her feet touched just because the neighbour's child died a few months ago from an accident with the binding. Besides, she has not fed or looked after her two younger brothers this morning!'

A small whimpering voice protested 'But I had to wash the clothes first ….'

Yiling tried to soothe the irate mother and explain that she should not have the child's feet bound, for who else would do the household chores and look after the family? Her daughter would not be able to do all that if her feet were bound. The mother was unconvinced. At close range, Yiling saw that the woman could be no more than two years older than she, yet a fourth child was due! Yiling offered a small sum of money, although she knew it was only a temporary solution.

Yiling emerged from the shack to find Bao and the girl laughing together. Bao had given her the cookie he had taken from home in case he got hungry.

The incident left Yiling unsettled. She felt for the little girl, who she learnt from Bao was named Peng Peng. Yiling was troubled by the mother's air of self-righteousness. Poverty did not necessarily teach a person empathy, compassion or humility. It could, in fact, harden their hearts!

Yiling wanted to check on the family, A week later she and Bao were there again. Bao had brought cookies and was laughing with Peng in the corner, sharing the food with the two little brothers. Peng's mother had given birth the night before, so the father was home that morning. Seng was a pleasant young man who bowed deeply to Yiling, for Peng had told him everything, including about the monetary gift. He had been happy that the latest child was a healthy female, although his wife had wanted more boys. Yiling learnt that Seng was a farm worker paid by the day. He had to leave early and return at sunset, coming home to a cold frugal meal and chores too strenuous for his young daughter. His was a true love story of two teenagers from peasant stock.

Yiling made a decision. The young man was strong and able to work at the Duke's residence. The large garden at the back could do with more attention. She could have the peonies and plum blossoms she had wanted to plant for years.

Yiling told Seng that he should stay home for a few days. He was to report at the Duke's residence in a week's time for his new job and to bring Peng with him. She was to train as a new maid. With her small salary and his better pay, they could afford for his wife to employ a peasant woman to help with the two boys and the newborn daughter. He would be able to leave home later in the morning and get home earlier, giving him more time with his family. It was an arrangement that would make life easier for the family.

It was never Yiling's plan to train Peng as a maid. She would be more like a daughter. She was to be educated and brought up as a child from a well-to-do family. Yiling did not realise it then, but she had saved the first of many children from foot binding and begun her charity work.

18

The Legend of the Young Lovers at the Great Wall

The voice of the pretty seventeen year old Yeen penetrated the late morning air. It was a clear sweet voice that told of happiness:

'The mountains are calling, the mountains are calling.
Blue green they stand majestic
Beneath a sky so blue,
But when the moon is supreme
Shinning down at the village
Nestled at the bottom of the mountains
The heavens produce a scene of rare beauty
Oh, of beauty incomparable ...'

It was an old traditional song but the young maiden felt it had been written for her village. Yeen's village was hidden in the mountains. The temperature was always cool, the days and nights beautiful and the villagers thankful and happy.

As she crossed a little bridge Yeen could see her handsome lover, Pei, waving to her. He called out 'I heard you, I heard you!' They ran to embrace and their happiness filled the air. Pei was a year older than Yeen. They had been betrothed for months and their wedding was only two days away.

Yeen's father had passed away when she was fifteen, leaving her the house and a slim gold ring. She sorely felt his loss, as he had brought her up alone from the time she was ten, providing so much love that she needed no one else.

It was fortunate that Yeen had met the tall, smiling youth who lived at the far end of the village. The attraction was mutual. She knew that he was the one she would love forever! Her father's gold band became her gift to Pei. She looked around her wooden house, a little sad to be selling it. Yeen would be living in the larger house with her husband and father-in-law, Yu, a man much like her father, with so much love to give.

Yeen had been taught to sew by her mother and had a talent for it. Word spread of the gifted needlewoman and villagers approached her to do work for them. Yeen's fees for mending were modest and she was popular with her sweet face and ready smile. She also sewed new garments for those who could afford it, enabling her to save a little nest egg. With the sale of her humble childhood home her nest egg grew considerably.

Pei was an accomplished carpenter, having learnt the trade from an uncle. He also did wood carvings, and made an excellent figure of a rabbit for Yeen's previous birthday. It sent her into raptures. She swore that she would carry it with her for the rest of her life. It was the same with the "mountain" song. She would sing that song only for him, no one else. Sometimes Pei would be called to the richer families in the village to build a new room, cupboards, furniture or even help build a new home. The newly married couple were saving steadily.

Each morning Yeen worked at her sewing in the village, returning for lunch to her new home. She would sing her special song as she crossed the little bridge. There at the other end stood her tall young husband with his ready smile. They walked home arm in arm, pink cheeked and flushed, welcomed at the doorway of their home by Yu. He cooked for them. He was no mean cook and they ate well. In the village they were known as "the happy threesome".

What an idyllic life!

But life is unpredictable and happiness fleeting. Someone from the village who wanted to make his fortune had travelled down to the towns in the lowlands. He met a captain at a fortress town. Wishing to ingratiate himself he told of his hometown in the mountains said there were many strong young men who would make good soldiers.

Not much later, the captain received orders that they needed workers, as the Great Wall was in need of repair and strengthening. The fortune hunter from the remote village led the captain through the foothills to the village.

The young couple had been married for two months and were having a late lunch with Yu. Yes, the happy threesome. Suddenly the captain and his soldiers burst into the room. He showed his badge and the imperial decree to recruit men. The soldiers seemed annoyed that these villagers were eating well. They pushed the old man aside, grabbed Pei and ignored the young wife's pleas to allow them to say goodbye. Yeen begged to know where they were taking her husband, receiving a curt reply that he would be working at the Great Wall.

Yu and Yeen were left in anguish. Neither of them knew that such grief was possible. Something had been ripped from within them. But while Yeen still hoped for future reunion, Yu understood that he would never see his son again. There had not been enough time to even make a little one! He despaired. He had a fine daughter-in-law but his family line was dead. Yu hurled his family tablet and incense burner into the garden. He lost the will to live. In the early mornings Yeen would find him standing in his thin bedclothes looking at the sky asking 'WHY?' She would lead him back to bed and return to the kitchen to prepare some congee for him.

Yeen continued with her sewing work to support herself and her father-in-law, remaining convinced that she would see her husband again. She decided she would make him a quilted jacket, for she heard it was cold at the Great Wall. She searched for heavier pieces of cloth that gave greater warmth. She was going to make a patchwork jacket with darker colour patches at the edges. Her hours at home were spent sorting out the pieces of cloth and sewing them together at night by candlelight. Working on the jacket gave her some purpose in life.

Walking home there was no longer a tall figure waiting for her at the other side of the bridge. Yeen wished with all her heart that the figure would materialise, but it was not to be. She did not sing any more.

Yu now had a chest infection, was often coughing and no longer did the cooking. Yeen would bring home medicinal herbs from the village, at least able to relieve his coughing. She brewed the medicine and cooked congee for them both. At nightfall she returned to her sewing by candlelight. Looking at the quilt as it took shape gave her some solace.

Yu's coughing worsened, as expected. It was perhaps a strange scene to behold. There was understanding and love between the old man and his son's wife. There was little need for words as their eyes settled on each other. They were united in their great love for the missing Pei. Each day was hard, but there was some joy in seeing the quilt near completion. Then one day the old man called for her. He told her he was going and that the three of them would be together in a future world. Yu thanked Yeen for her care and love, not only for him, but for his son. He said goodbye. That night there was little coughing and he was dead in the morning.

The young woman dipped into her savings and arranged a decent burial for Yu. She thanked the neighbours who came to pay their last respects. On the night after the funeral Yeen returned to working on the quilted jacket when a strange thing happened: the needle went into her finger and drew blood. Although it was not serious it had not happened before.

At exactly the same moment was a cry at a section of the Great Wall. It came from an emaciated tall figure. He spoke softly into the darkness. 'My beloved wife, I can hold on no more. Forgive me. The pain in my chest is over powering. I know I will see you in the next world. Goodbye, my love.'

Back in the village, Yeen knew what was ahead of her. Her father-in-law was gone and there was no reason to stay. She sold off the house cheaply, knowing she would never return. She was going to search for her husband. She was going to the Great Wall. Yeen took one last look around the room, lifted the large cloth bag bearing the quilt, her wooden rabbit, a soft warm blanket, her savings and a few pieces of dry flat bread and a little water. The wide strap of the bag rested across her collar bones, the bulk behind her, leaving her hands free should she need to climb. She walked with her head held high, crossed the bridge and out of the village on the journey in search of her husband.

Yeen arrived at the first of the lowland towns and bought some of the steamed buns she loved. She asked for directions to the nearest section of the Great Wall. At the third town she bumped into a young man who did not watch where he was going.

Yeen was astonished. It was the man who brought the captain and his soldiers to her village, to her house. Without hesitation she told him that she was going to the Wall to search for her husband. Was it guilt that made him offer to help her? They trudged for days along the foot hills to the nearest section of the Wall. As soon as they reached their goal he said a quick goodbye and scooted off.

She walked along the Wall, approaching workers, soldiers and whoever she met, asking if they had seen a tall young man with a fair complexion and a mole near his right eye. Finally, someone said he had seen such a person many months ago. He had been sent to the next section of the Wall. So off she went to the next section many days' walk away.

At the next section she was told to keep going. She sat down for a longish rest, taking a good drink and clearing her throat. Out of her lips came the sweet song she had not sung since the day her husband was taken from her.

'The mountains are calling, the mountains are calling …' In fact, it was Yeen was calling for her husband. Her voice was still clear and pure, although now tinged with an unmistakable sadness. It was so beautiful that all who heard stopped to listen. Many a person told her 'Little sister you sing beautifully.' Others offered to help her. But she moved on alone.

Yeen lost any sense of time. Offered both food and water by the workers and soldiers on the Wall, she ate to pacify the hunger pangs, drinking only from thirst and the need to clear her throat.

By now Yeen no longer had her pink complexion and healthy build, becoming a tired, almost ragged figure. She travelled from one section of the wall to the next. She was getting weaker, yet her voice remained strong, and her strong will kept her pushing onwards. Yeen knew she would find Pei.

After what might have been months, if not years, Yeen arrived at a new section of the Wall and sensed she was near her journey's end. Although exhausted and wasted from her long search, Yeen found a new strength and sang her best. In the cold night air and under the beauty of the stars, her sweet voice rang true and clear. Seemingly in response was a rumble and a small explosion. A section of the Wall blew open. There was much fear among the workers, but Yeen headed straight to where the explosion took place. She knew what to do. Yeen had called and Pei had heard and answered.

Yeen made her way through the dust and rubble, finding the long skeleton lying there. To Yeen it was not a set of bones, for she saw the image of her young husband smiling at her. The remains of his clothes were disintegrating, but the stitching on the shirt was her very own neat handiwork. There, too, around the neck of the skeleton was a string on which a thin gold band hung. It was the one her father left her and she had given to Pei. From her cloth bag she pulled out the patchwork quilt jacket. She placed it over his skeleton and lay down next to him.

Yeen had reached her journey's end. She had found Pei and accomplished what she had set out to do. She had found her true love again and would keep him warm. Yeen closed her eyes, never to open them again. She was at peace and slept the forever sleep.

19

At the Great Wall of China

Hoong was indeed lucky not to be sent to the Great Wall as a labourer, but as an officer accompanied by Batir and the twins. He was incredibly lucky to be accompanied by his Flying Horsemen. This meant he was an officer of some importance. It also showed that General Wan and the Minister of War and Defence were not without clout in Beijing. Greater good fortune he could not ask for when he learnt that the commander of that section of the Great Wall outside Beijing, Commander Ho, had formerly served as an officer under General Wan. Ho was among the new breed of patriots, one who wanted the best for his country. It meant Hoong had someone he could comfortably work with. Perhaps Fate was doing its best for Hoong to make up for what was taken from him.

It was during the early months at the Wall that Batir told Hoong the truth about Yiling. Batir said he had seen her that morning when they marched through Jian'an. His spy reported that she was married to a powerful duke and they had a child. Batir had not told him in case Hoong threw caution aside and rushed to see her.

Batir saw the joy that showed on Hoong's face, but also the despair that took over the next moment. The old duke could still give Yiling a child but he, Hoong, could never provide her with family. He was no longer a man. He could offer her nothing. He could only keep his love for Yiling within him. But at least he had known love, while many others had not been as fortunate! Batir understood Hoong's pain.

Batir also marvelled at how Hoong had kept his physique, unlike so many eunuchs. He was an impressive tall figure, with a sinewy and magnificent body. His voice was firm and low. Batir had heard that eunuchs were known to smell of urine, for their "waterworks" had been damaged, but knew that Hoong was meticulously clean. He swam whenever he had the opportunity, having been taught by Batir himself! Hoong was known to have a taste for bathing in the local hot water springs, never being deterred by the smell of sulphur.

Hoong's lack of involvement with women made some wonder if he could be more inclined towards men. Particularly women, who could not believe that their charms did not work on him.

Hoong's assignment was at the most important part of the Wall, for it was just outside Beijing, the seat of Ming power. It took no more than an hour to communicate with the Court from there. The timing was also perfect, for the state coffers were overflowing and the Emperor willing to spend on the country's defences, despite his fixation on the treasure fleet. Hoong's orders were not only to reinforce and strengthen the Wall but to introduce innovations.

Hoong realised that it was not a straightforward matter of just building a wall. The terrain was mountainous. There was a need for engineering skills, for planners with intelligence, manpower and a constant supply of bricks. Higher and stronger walls were required, so too watch towers and beacons. They needed an improved system of signals so that information on the size of the invading forces, their speed, strength and direction could be included. He had learnt much while stationed in Hu and already thought of building double walls to deceive invading forces into thinking they had broken through, only to find that they were trapped and faced death. Hoong also had thoughts of secret tunnels. Besieging forces could be taken by surprise at night and destroyed by the Ming forces!

Authority was not everything. How to manage it was even more important. Hoong had learnt humility from his mother, Yin. Her own mother had died when she was only ten, leaving her in the care of her father, an impoverished scholar and a humble man. Yin learnt to be aware of others and was thankful for the kindness they received. Hoong knew his skills and authority were recognised by Commander Ho, but also that he should not assume too much. And yet, changes were needed.

Hoong approached the Commander for a private conversation. He explained that he was there not to criticise but to help bring changes for the better. He asked to be corrected when he was wrong. This cleared the air, making it easy for the two to work together.

But the first requirement was a capable labour supply.

Labour came from local villagers, prisoners and criminals, as well as political dissidents from Beijing. The overseer used his whip freely, "as it made the workers agreeable". Hoong soon found that someone was cutting the workers' rations. He strongly believed it was impossible to work without enough food. The problems were traced to the overseer, who was feathering his nest in preparation for retirement.

Hoong added a large amount of his own funds to hurry the man to a happy early retirement. Having no dependents and few expenses, Hoong was never averse to helping when he could. Consequently, a sickly, demoralised work force became a healthier one.

Hoong learnt much from workers at the Wall.

The Stories of Wei, Woo and Uxi

On his sixth day at the Wall Hoong met the scholar Wei. Hoong was making his early rounds when a staggering figure almost crashed into him, collapsing at his feet. A soldier supervisor, one of the many in charge of the builders, was chasing him with a whip. The soldier told Hoong as he bowed that he had whipped the man for refusing to work. Hoong had a quick look at the collapsed worker, noticing that his soft white hands were bleeding. Most interesting! Hoong ordered that the man be fed, cleaned and brought to him in his private room.

Later that day Hoong returned to his room to find the man waiting for him and heard his story. The scholar Wei had never been faced with manual labour. He was the only son of a poet, a family of landed gentry. Wei was preparing for the imperial examination in Beijing. He was expected to be successful and recruited into the bureaucracy. At the least, he would be appointed a magistrate. But his uncle, who had his eyes on the family estates, felt it was the right time to strike before Wei succeeded at the imperial examination. Wei's poet father was accused of being a traitor and hauled off to the local court, where the honest, dreamy poet admitted that he did associate with a Jurchen.

As a young man, Wei's father had been saved from drowning by a young Jurchen tribesman. This happened on the one occasion he had ventured outside the city walls with family members, including the stepbrother who made the accusation. A bond had formed between the two young men. The Jurchen had visited him, although it had been unwise to continue the friendship. Wei's father was too honest to deny that he had associated with a Jurchen and that was sufficient evidence against him.

As he was a poet of some standing, his sentence was not execution but to be sent to the Great Wall for hard labour. A chest infection brought him death before the sentence was executed. Wei found that he was to take his father's place. Many things had changed for the better in the modern Ming dynasty, but not the system of justice. A crime, even unproven, committed by a member of the family could mean execution of the whole family, even an entire clan or village!

Hoong decided that this talented scholar with the soft hands should not be sent back as a labourer to the Wall. It would be ridiculous, the quality of his work and his productivity being so poor. There was a need for his talents. A well-educated man could send first class reports back to Beijing, not only on tribal activity at the Great Wall, but also on a host of other issues: on the state of the defences, administration, expenses and a hundred related matters. Hoong's fortress could now boast of a top scholar on top of everything else.

Through Wei, Hoong discovered that there was another scholar amongst the builders: Woo, who, unlike Wei, had strong hands. He was not interested in the classics, but in calculations.

One of Hoong's current projects was the unsatisfactory supply of bricks. Transporting them took even more time than laying them. Building kilns at the base of the Wall solved one problem, the help of nearby villagers solved others. Woo was put in charge of bricks. He calculated the number of bricks required at the building sites. It was Woo who suggested establishing friendly relations with the villagers and giving them pride and honour by allowing them to put the names of the villagers and workers on a simple plaque on the Wall itself.

Hoong also found an outstanding village youth who seemed to have been born with engineering skills.

Hoong's keen eyes had noticed a youth often kicking the bricks laid the day before. Was he assessing their strength? Then he would look out into the distance. Was he thinking about where the Wall should continue? Hoong questioned him and nearly fell over when he found that was exactly what the young man had on his mind! Hoong had discovered Uxi, the engineer with the amazing intellect and vision.

20

Skirmishes at the Great Wall

Three years passed. Hoong was busy with constructing additions to the Wall. He had spent much time with Woo and Uxi. The regular supply of high quality bricks from the nearby kilns was a great improvement. Much was due to the endless efforts of Woo. But a greater achievement was the contribution of Uxi, who worked out where to place the new sections of the Wall. Older sections were not merely joined up, but rebuilt and strengthened. Was it a surprise that time passed quickly?

Hoong never forgot he was a warrior first, and that his battle skills were responsible for this assignment at the Great Wall. Throughout the three years, while planning and construction took up much of his time, he made sure the early mornings were spent maintaining and improving his battle skills. A strong Ming army kept the marauding tribes at bay.

At the first rays of sunlight Hoong and Batir were outside the Wall with their Flying Horsemen, cantering out to the open plains. Even Commander Ho enjoyed watching the various manoeuvres the group practised. Attacking as one solid unit, splitting up into two, forming a circle to surround the enemy. As always, the speed and swivelling of the upper body and the shooting action of the bow and arrow were a delight to watch. There was the use of whistles and hand gestures to change direction. Many pairs of eyes watched from the fortress walls as if it was the morning's entertainment.

Small groups of tribesmen often appeared but departed as Hoong and his men came out. Occasionally a tribe would challenge them. There were skirmishes but no real threats. Indeed, it was a shock for the tribesmen to see that there were two leaders followed by horsemen who could move as fast, if not faster, than them. Plus, there was still the mighty Ming Cavalry to contend with, as well as the cannons on the fortress walls.

News had spread that the fair-skinned, slightly Mongol-looking warrior and darker, pure Mongol warrior were a formidable pair to take on. It somehow also became known that Hoong's mother and grandmother were Han Chinese. The soldiers at the fortress accepted him as their own, notwithstanding his Mongol heritage. Soon Batir was rumoured to have Chinese blood!

Hoong was so active each day that he slept soundly each night. His private thoughts were locked away. When he had time he studied his precious copy of Sun Tze's *The Art of War*.

An Important Encounter at the Great Wall

Early in the fourth year at the Wall things started to happen.

Just before dawn there was commotion at the western gates of the fortress. Two scouts had ridden through the night. Hoong was already awake and at the gates immediately. The scouts had just dismounted and the horses still slippery with sweat and foaming at the mouth. He gave orders that the scouts be fed and rested before reporting in full.

It transpired that three tribes had combined under a strong leader. Shades of Genghis Khan and the Yuan dynasty! The information was hurried to Beijing, but before return instructions were received, a messenger from the tribes arrived, asking to speak to the commander of the fortress. The Commander was informed that the tribes would set up camp in the distance. In the late afternoon a dust storm was seen to be gathering. The enemy had arrived.

Soon a lone rider approached with a white flag and the message that their leader wanted to meet the Mongol Chinese warrior who was often seen exercising his group of horsemen. The warrior who led the skirmishes against the tribes. Commander Ho knew they wanted Hoong. Hoong had no hesitation about riding to the enemy encampment, although Ho feared it could be a trap to kill his strongest warrior and right hand man.

Hoong asked to be given an hour by himself. He thought deep and hard. Do the tribes really want war? Or the politicians at the imperial court? Many had little experience of war, knowing only of the fame and glory that victory brings. Hoong was realistic enough to know that negotiation was the only way to avoid an unnecessary conflict.

Looking around him, Hoong saw the faces of the young soldiers, the ones that he had trained to shoot their arrows from horseback. Then too, the stationary archers with the heavier bows who lined the fortress. There were the foot soldiers who would bow with respect whenever he passed them. Down to the gunners who stood ready to fire the cannons, although there had been little use of them in recent times. They never failed to greet Assistant Commander Hoong. All life mattered.

Hoong never forgot the teachings of Sun Tze: "know thy enemy". Going out to the camping tribesmen would allow Hoong to learn about them. Yes, he would go. It was worth the risk. He wanted to go alone, but Batir insisted on accompanying him, and so the brave pair rode out of the fortress gates, leaving behind a very anxious commander.

They rode untroubled to the large tribal encampment, where they were taken to a large, imposing ger in the midst of smaller ones.

A youngish Jurchen leader greeted them. He was only a little older than Hoong. He spoke in a clear voice that sounded familiar to Hoong. Hoong listened as he was congratulated for his courage in coming to the camp. The leader said he had seen Hoong and Batir during the skirmishes outside the fortress but had not directly fought them.

'Wait a minute – I know that voice', thought Hoong, hearing in his mind the words 'Anu, Anu, wait for me'. He suddenly recalled the memory's source. 'Are you not the young warrior who followed tribal leader Anu years ago outside the fortress at Hu'xinzhou?' The young leader smiled. 'You remember me! I am Abu.'

Abu relaxed and invited Hoong and Batir to be seated, for he had matters to discuss with them.

Abu said he would be honest. He had asked for Hoong because he felt he was trustworthy. The tribesmen may be bloodthirsty at war but they were not without virtue, morals or principles. Abu explained their predicament.

The previous two winters had been unusually severe. Many old Jurchens and babies had died. The soldiers were undernourished, for they were short of grain, but worse, the livestock had been depleted and they were short of meat. The animals, including the horses, did not have good grazing pastures. The two other tribes had suffered the same fate. If they had grain and livestock there was no need for war. They had little choice but to battle and plunder. They were desperate.

Yes, thought Hoong, the last two winters had been uncommonly harsh. Before that the harvests had been bountiful and a strong Ming government had hoarded supplies of grain. There was feed for the livestock and food for the citizens. At the fortress the soldiers had enough food, as well as plenty of firewood and charcoal burners for warmth behind the walls.

Silence fell. Abu thought about his failing baby nephew and his father's last breaths as he lay dying in bed. Hoong remembered Sun Tze's words on war: "The greatest victory is that which requires no battle."

Hoong now knew his foe's weakness. They were not at their peak. They were not well nourished, but did China want war? The Ming troops were strong but … desperation could give the tribesmen the edge. There would be death on both sides.

Hoong knew the Chinese government had supplies to spare. He could appeal to General Wan and the Minister of War and Defence. This solution would mean keeping the men at the fortress safe and intact. Perhaps for more desperate times in the future.

Hoong considered that Abu could be trusted. He told Abu that he thought he could persuade Beijing to provide supplies of grain and livestock. He asked Abu for time to organise it all.

Back at the fortress he told Commander Ho what had taken place. The Commander agreed with Hoong completely. He had seen too much death. Together they sent their appeal to General Wan and the Minister of War and Defence.

For once there was little questioning or opposition from Beijing. Hoong, Commander Ho and all at the fortress could not believe the speed at which the requested supplies arrived. They were astonished. None cared to know the reason for the good fortune!

Abu arrived with a small detachment to collect the supplies and livestock. They had brought many bags of furs with them. Abu was a man of honour. He would pay for what he received.

Controversy Follows Hoong's Negotiated Peace

Hoong's negotiated peace was greeted with much acclaim at the fortress and by General Wan and the Minister of War and Defence in Beijing. Many a soldier greeted Hoong with tears in his eyes. They knew that large scale war with the aggressive barbarian tribes meant death for many, as well as serious injury. Few would escape unscathed. The older soldiers had seen death too often.

Orders arrived for Hoong to meet the new Emperor in Beijing. It was this Emperor who had agreed to negotiations and rapidly send out the requested supplies. The Emperor had been in an unusually good mood because of Admiral Zheng He's triumphant return from Africa, bringing back gold, precious stones and a giraffe, amongst other gifts. Rulers from three of the lands visited pledged loyalty and annual tribute. It meant that the recent "treasure fleet" expenses were covered.

The young emperor had been spending an early morning with his pet giraffe when Hoong's request arrived.

Hoong took Batir with him to the capital, where he was welcomed by General Wan and the Minister. They were happy to inform him that Prince Yen had become the new emperor. The death of the sickly heir to the throne, the Prime Minister's son-in-law, had solved many problems. Wan warned Hoong that his negotiated peace had not been welcomed by everyone. Many in the Prime Minister's faction questioned why the barbarians had not been annihilated when the Ming army was so strong!

Hoong believed he had done the right thing and had no regrets. He followed Sun Tze's teachings. He accepted that there would always be people with different views, as well as those who had little understanding of war.

The Minister informed Hoong that the Emperor wanted to meet him the next day for a private audience. He was invited to stay at the sumptuous royal guest lodge. Hoong declined the offer. He preferred the large guest quarters of General Wan, where he had stayed before. He had felt comfortable there. He asked the General to allow Batir to accompany him.

A tired but happy Hoong retired to a large room and Batir to a smaller adjoining room at the General's guest quarters. He wanted a good night's sleep, as he had been promised a tour of the new palace, the Forbidden City. He had heard the Forbidden City was one of its kind, the largest, most lavish palace ever built.

An Assassination Attempt

Hoong blew out the candles next to his bed. Darkness reigned, but figures moved across the courtyard outside the bedrooms. Were they waiting for Batir to quench the light of his candles? Batir's keen ears picked up the sound of a pebble being kicked on the pathway. There was an intruder! Batir had not yet undressed. A cold shiver ran through his body. Hoong was in danger. Batir still carried his knife in his belt. He also grabbed the sword from the table and dashed into Hoong's room.

Hoong had just fallen asleep. Years of military training alerted him to the danger, but this time he was too late. He awoke to see a pair of cold eyes staring into his. Hoong thought he was about to die and expected the pain of a dagger piercing his heart. Instead, he heard a gurgling sound as the black-robed assassin fell onto him. 'Hoong, are you alright?' Batir had been a fraction faster, plunging his knife deep into the assassin first. Batir was also a dangerous man in his prime, one trained to kill!

Two more attackers charged into Hoong's room, but now there were two armed fighting men to contend with, Hoong and Batir. Soon there were three dead assassins in the room!

The sound of fighting in the courtyard was followed by Wan's angry voice asking his private guards whether they were sleeping pigs or fighting men. There had been another three men in black, killed by the General's guards. An assassination had almost succeeded. The men hung their heads in shame while Hoong reassured the General.

The next morning, at the close of a session, Hoong was escorted into the Court by the Minister of War and Defence. In good times with strong emperors there were always court sessions. The grandeur of the scene was beyond anything Hoong could ever imagine! In the imperial courtroom were huge red pillars. Spiralling up the pillars were dragons cast in gold. An elaborate throne rested on a raised stage at the end of the large hall. Its magnificence made it quite clear who it was for. Into the room came an orderly crowd of people dressed in grand official robes and head dresses designating their rank. They were in red, blue and green.

On each side of the throne stood two intimidating military figures in armour. All talking ceased when the trumpets sounded and a voice called out that the Emperor had arrived. Everyone except the military guard fell to the ground in obeisance. The Emperor walked to his throne to the cheers of 'May the Emperor live a thousand years.' The Emperor sat on the throne and gestured to the assembly to rise.

Hoong was not intimidated by the scene, even though he was seeing it for first time. It brought a smile to his face, as he found it most interesting!

Military matters were presented first, thanks to the Minister of War and Defence. A fully armoured figure stepped forward to report that there was peace in the country, no riots, no rebellions in Outer China. He reminded the assembly that the border with the barbarian tribes was long and there were the usual skirmishes in the east and north but no major problems. In the northwest, across the Gobi Desert to Dunhuang, there was peace. In the south, the Grand Canal had successfully enabled the transport of food supplies to relieve the drought there. In short, all was well.

The Minister stepped forward, announcing there was a person whom he wished to present to the Court. Someone who had benefited the empire by avoiding an expensive war. Perhaps the Minister was trying to remind all that they owe much to the military. Hoong's name was announced and he came forward to show himself. There was much applause.

Then out stepped a junior minister, loudly declaring that he had something to say. He accused Hoong of complicity and cowardice. Hoong should have gone to war and destroyed the enemy. That every-one knew how strong the Ming army was and that the menace of the barbarian tribes could have been removed forever. Next the smooth talker alleged that the negotiated peace had been costly. Hoong had given away grain and livestock unnecessarily during years of poor harvests. The junior minister grossly exaggerated the costs, but the enemies of the military clearly had first class spies, for they knew so much.

At this juncture the Minister of War and Defence signalled that he wished to speak once more. He had something to show the Emperor. His soldiers emptied two large bags onto the floor. Out came furs of a variety, standard and beauty few people had seen before! Sable, mink, deer, fox, marten, raccoon dog ... Abu, the tribal leader, had given the best furs his tribe had accumulated over many years, for he placed the lives of his people above material things.

Even those who had experience with furs were stunned, including the Prime Minister, who knew his wife and daughters would give anything to have one of these furs around their shoulders! Many knew that the collection would have cost more than the grain and livestock given to the tribes. There were no more challenges. The Minister and Hoong left with their heads held high.

Afterwards, Hoong's private audience with the Emperor went well. The Emperor treated him as an old friend. He had not forgotten the time when Hoong carried him up from the pit, the incident several years ago during the royal hunt. He remembered the strong shoulders against which he lay helpless and the smell of Hoong's sweat.

Hoong explained why he negotiated peace rather than fight. There were no real winners in war. The Ming troops were strong but Hoong wanted them to live another day. China shared a very long border with the tribes. It was not possible to eradicate them all. The Emperor told Hoong that he, too, had studied Sun Tze. He would avoid war when that was possible. He explained that, as an emperor, he had a delicate job of balancing the rival factions, that he often had to act dumb!

The Emperor insisted on giving a banquet to thank Hoong for saving him when he was a prince and for his contributions to his country as a military commander. Hoong's attempts at refusal were met by the Emperor's promise to keep the party small and private.

21

Princess Min Min

The Forbidden City, like all royal residences, was a dangerous place, anything but a happy environment in which to live.

Princess Min Min was fathered by the previous emperor in his old age. In fact, she shared the same mother with the new emperor. Their mother was the old emperor's favourite, but her life in the palace was miserable. The Princess had the same sad eyes as her mother and the same simple nature, with no love for intrigue or manipulation. She'd had her first bleeding two years before, so was ready to wed. But when her brother said she could have any eligible man in his empire, she replied that she was interested neither in men nor in marriage.

Min Min was lucky in that her brother, ten years older, adored her, as he did their mother. He protected her so she was able to lead a quiet life in a remote corner of the new Forbidden City, attending only the smaller imperial gatherings. She was invited to the private banquet for Hoong, since her brother thought she would enjoy it.

That evening she wondered why the palace ladies were so excited about the warrior in whose honour the banquet was. As she walked to the banquet hall she saw her brother talking to someone. Well-formed muscular shoulders above a broad back faced her, turning as the Emperor greeted his sister.

Min Min stood transfixed, as if struck by a lightning bolt. It was not merely his noble posture and good looks. There was something special about him that appealed to her. It was the first time she felt she might want a man in her life. She now understood the whispers of her cousins when they spoke in awe about men they found attractive!

Perhaps love or simply attraction made her bold. It was a surprised Emperor who heard 'Is this your honoured guest?' Hoong was also surprised and looked at the pretty young lady. His eyes lingered on her face as he took in the sad eyes that resembled Yiling's. The Emperor noticed the reaction between the two.

The dinner was of the best dishes from the royal kitchen. It had been years since Hoong tasted the Chinese delicacies. He could do without fine food but it did not mean he did not welcome it. He also appreciated the textures and the sauces that teased his taste buds. The clever use of vinegar and spices added to the experience.

After the magnificent meal came the entertainment. Hoong would have preferred an acrobatic performance, but one had been seen at the palace recently, so they had the greatest dance troupe in the country. The young dancers were agile and moved without apparent effort. The audience applauded their fluid and graceful performance. Hoong was reminded of the tribal dances of the young girls he had seen in the past. As Hoong watched the dancers he was watched by the Princess. She was not going to allow him to disappear from her life!

As the evening came to an end the Princess approached the men. She asked her brother whether Commander Hoong could join them for their morning walk around the garden and fish pond in the grounds of the Forbidden City. The Emperor readily agreed, seeing Min Min's intensity.

Hoong spent a most pleasant morning with the Emperor and the Princess. The Emperor was pleased to see the uplifted spirits of his sister. He had promised himself years ago that he would look after her and her happiness was his priority.

The following day Princess Min Min sent word to her brother that she needed to see him urgently.

She wished to marry Hoong and wanted her brother to make it possible. The Emperor had already considered the possibility. Having a military hero by his side could be an advantage, but he would have to consult his advisers. Hoong's military superior General Wan came to mind immediately. The General was summoned.

It was no surprise to General Wan that the subject was Hoong. Nor was he surprised that the Emperor's sister was smitten. Wan was not blind to Hoong's unusually good looks. His own daughter had fallen for Hoong some five years ago and that was after only seeing him twice.

Wan had to reveal to his daughter Hoong's secret. She was his only remaining child, as his two sons had died as young boys. Even if Hoong was willing, there could be no grandchildren. He knew how unhappy his daughter had been. For a whole year she hardly came out of her room. He visited her often, reminding her that she was his sole surviving child and she had a filial duty to him. To give him grandchildren. Finally she emerged again and met someone, in three years giving him three grandchildren on whom he doted!

General Wan knew he had to tell Hoong's secret to the Emperor. Hoong was a eunuch, castrated at the age of fourteen as a prisoner of war. The Emperor could hardly believe his ears. Surely it was not possible. He looked every inch a virile male! Was it because he was already physically developed when he was castrated or was he a most extraordinary case?

The Emperor told his sister the terrible truth. Her reply was disbelief. And regardless, she still wanted to marry Hoong and thought that he had some feelings for her. She did not need children, only his presence. She could survive on whatever affection he would give her.

General Wan also related the case of his love struck daughter. The Emperor passed on this story to his unheeding sister.

Princess Min Min threatened suicide if her brother did not grant her wish. The Emperor felt that Hoong was the only person who could talk sense into her. Hoong was summoned.

To the gardens Hoong came. It was a place of beauty, the result of much work and ingenuity. No one else was visible until Princess Min

Min emerged from the shadows. She had watched Hoong narrowing his eyes at the early morning sun, detecting a degree of sadness on his serious face. Could any female not feel for this man?

The Princess made a slight noise and he turned to face her, a slow smile lighting up his features. She led him to a pavilion where there were seats, tea and dainty little cookies. Her eyes were swollen from crying, her face sad. She blurted out that she loved him and wished to spend the rest of her life with him.

Hoong considered his words for a few moments then asked her to listen carefully to what he had to say.

Hoong went straight to the core of the matter.

'Do you understand that there is no future with me, Princess? I can never give you children. I am a eunuch and a soldier. My work is to defend the country. I will be gone for long periods of time doing what I am trained for. There is every chance I will not return from battle. You cannot follow me and you would have no children to provide you with company and love. You do not deserve such a life.

'And my heart belongs to someone I have loved for a long time. No one can displace her!'

Perhaps it was those last words that hit her hardest. He loved someone else.

In those moments Min Min understood her situation. She had been pampered for all her sixteen years. She had survived because of her brother. She would be a liability to Hoong. And worst, Hoong's heart was with another.

After some moments of silence, Min Min raised her head and looked into his eyes. 'Perhaps you can give me a goodbye hug?' she quietly asked.

They stood up. His arms went around her. Her arms reached round his back. She could feel his muscles as she clung to him. She closed her eyes to lock in those moments, which she would remember forever! Her mind said 'The next lifetime, perhaps.' Maybe she would be lucky enough to have him in her next existence. She sighed. Hoong gently extricated himself. The Princess watched as he disappeared from her life.

The Emperor came out from the bushes, from where he had seen all. He saw the resolute look on Min Min's face joining the sad eyes. She had grown up. She had accepted her fate.

22

Hoong's New Appointment

Hoong returned to his work at the Great Wall. The fortnight at Beijing had been more than enough for him. The same day he left Princess Min Min at the Forbidden City he made tracks for "home", riding through the night to the fortress on the Wall. After a few hours' sleep he was exercising with Batir, who had returned some days earlier. Venturing onto the open ground beyond the fortress with his Flying Horsemen always made him feel alive. Both he and Batir liked nothing better than the speed and cold morning air.

By this time they had trained the twins to work with the mobile archers. The twins were officers with his Flying Horsemen and were well capable of managing them. Nevertheless, Hoong felt that either he or Batir should be with the troops.

Back in Beijing, the General and the Minister of War and Defence had plans for Hoong's future. They were convinced that better use should be made of him. Hoong was an outstanding fighter, a leader and a military strategist. He should not be stationed in one place. They decided that Hoong should be given a new appointment as a special military adviser for the entire Great Wall across north-eastern China. He was to be given the power and funds to make improvements along that whole stretch once and for all.

Hoong accepted the appointment, but only on condition that his base remained at the fortress to where he could return regularly, and that he had the power to send Batir, the twins and close assistants to any point on the Wall if and when necessary.

This appointment was discussed at the imperial court. It had the Emperor's approval. Even the Prime Minister was sensible enough to know that Hoong was a rare talent not to be wasted. As long as he was not stationed in Beijing the Prime Minister felt comfortable.

For the next two years Hoong worked steadily, strengthening and reinforcing the Wall, rising to his challenges, while keeping an eye out for men of ability. His one great comfort was having Batir close to him. From time to time Batir left for some days. Batir would visit the fortress at Hu'xinzhou and check on the second group of Flying Horsemen. A capable Han Mongol captain was in charge of them. In fact, this captain was related to both Batir and Hoong. He was the grandson of Tolui's Mongol daughter. Hoong also knew Batir had a partner. Hoong never questioned, and Batir never said much. Batir felt any talk of women or family would hurt Hoong. However, if the subject was work they had much to say to each other!

23

Back to Yiling

From the time Yiling took Peng home to Duke Wu's residence, Bao changed from a sweet, quiet boy to a happy, chirpy one. It made Yiling feel she had made the right decision in employing Peng's father, Seng and taking Peng into her home.

She had told the Duke of her decision to employ Seng, apologising for taking the authority to do so. As usual, Wu supported her, for he trusted her judgment. Yiling knew she was indeed lucky to have him by her side.

Yiling watched Bao grow. It was definitely Hoong's jaw he had, as well as his eyes. She had been compensated in life by being given a miniature of the man she loved. The Duke also spent much time with him. Bao loved hearing the stories of the Duke's childhood, always showing great respect. Still, Yiling sensed that Bao thought the Duke was not his real father.

And each day when sunset came, the sad look in Yiling's eyes seemed more pronounced. It was the time when her thoughts turned to Hoong. Did he know she was still alive? Did he ever think of their days in the bamboo forest?

When they visited Peng's mother, Yiling could see the joy in Peng's face at the sight of her siblings. She always took along the little jar of cookies she saved up for her brothers. She would run to hold her baby sister. She would have loved to hug her mother had she been allowed to. She had so much love in her. But her mother had love only for her sons.

Yiling always brought fruit for the boys, for she knew their mother would not buy it. Fruit was good for them. Bao loved going along to play with the boys, who would rush to him, knowing he always brought them presents.

The family's financial circumstances had definitely improved. The boys wore better clothes and were cleaner. The paid help, a peasant woman, did her work well. Peng's mother looked less tired, no matter that she was still full of complaints. The baby girl, named Lili, was a greedy child who wanted to be fed all the time, and the mother's breasts were sore as a result. To Peng, six months old Lili was the cutest thing in the world, for her face was so round and chubby and her gurgles the most endearing sound.

Back at home, Yiling patiently sat through meals with the now ailing Duke. They dined in the main house, while Peng and Bao often ate in the kitchen. Yiling wanted the children to be free from adult strictures. She noticed that Peng was always rushing around doing things for Bao, and would always ensure that Bao had his food before she ate hers.

Peng would also carry Bao's things for him – his jacket, shoes, bits and pieces. Yiling did not want Bao growing up pampered. She took her son aside and told him he must not take advantage of Peng, that he should do things for himself.

"Mama, I would never hurt Peng", Bao protested. "I adored her since I saw her mother chasing her with the cane!"

The next day she saw Bao struggling with his little bag, jacket and shoes, for he would not allow Peng to carry them.

That afternoon Yiling was taught something by the children. She found them play acting in the garden. Engrossed in their own fun, they did not notice her. Bao pretended to be an old man, staggering along while Peng held his arm. Peng helped him to sit and started to wipe his brow. Suddenly Yiling knew what it was all about. They were imitating her and the Duke. The scene made Yiling realise how frail Wu had become.

A month later the Duke moved from their shared bedroom to the room next door. He was coughing at night and did not want to disturb Yiling. Yiling started brewing herbs that helped relieve his throat. She looked after him in the daytime and went back to her room at night to sleep.

The years passed. The Duke's mansion was vast and a schoolroom was set up a little distance from the main rooms. The Duke had been coaching Bao, for he knew so much of the literature and history of China, but it was time to have a full-time tutor. Peng was to study with Bao each morning. Yiling thought of Peng's two brothers. It would benefit them to join at least some of the sessions. Seng was overjoyed to have his children educated. Yiling decided to visit Peng's mother to explain the benefits of education, even if the boys ended up as craftsmen.

Yiling, Bao and Peng made their way to the house. As usual, Peng rushed to pick up her sister. Lili was almost three years old now. As soon as she saw Peng and Bao she cooed in delight, for they always brought cookies. The Duke's kitchen staff often baked cookies, so there were always snacks. Peng's mother was always pleasant, happy to receive the gifts.

Peng's mother seldom accepted advice, convinced she knew better. She was talking about having Lili's feet bound and marrying her off to a very rich family. She laughingly said if it was done really early Lili would have the smallest feet ever seen! The statement caused alarm, Peng's face turning pale and a cold shiver going through Yiling's body as she immediately thought of Lady Ee. Yiling felt that the child would have to be removed before any harm was done. Yiling also learned that the woman was pregnant again! She knew that Seng loved his wife dearly and found it hard to go against her wishes.

Seng, Peng and Yiling had a serious talk several days later. Seng would keep a close eye on Lili. They agreed that she must be taken away. Five was considered the youngest age for foot binding. But the mad woman of a mother might do it earlier. Lili was only a few days from her fourth birthday. Yiling decided she had to act as soon as she could. Luckily, the mother could be bribed. Yiling was willing to spend, but they still had to work out how to do it. Perhaps it was a fortunate that the mother had no special affection for her youngest child. She still referred to Lili as "the greedy thing" who would eat her out of house and home! Indeed, little Lili's favourite words were mumm, mumm, (food) and yumm, yumm (tasty).

Yiling knew she could never forgive herself if little Lili's feet were bound. After much thought she came up with a plan. Yiling offered to buy Seng and his wife a more expensive, larger home, with plenty of room for the boys. And a hamper filled with all the sweetmeats she loved would be there to welcome her when they moved in to the new house. Lili would move to the Duke's residence and share a room and bed with her sister. In short, she would be cared for by sister Peng.

The bribe worked, and Lili's mother reluctantly gave up her dream of having a daughter with the smallest feet in the country.

Then things seemed to happen all at once. Two days after Lili was settled at the Duke's mansion, Yiling found herself faced with the other issue that troubled her – abandoned women. On her way to the market with her maid, they were passing the middle income homes, the medium-sized brick homes with gardens. There was a woman on the roadside trying to cling to a man who was forcefully pushing her away. She appealed to him not to abandon her. She offered to work as a maid and not as the mistress. With a sneer he shouted at her. "What good are you? In three years you have not given me a child. I will have you thrashed with bamboo sticks by the servants if you turn up again. I have a new young concubine who pleasures me compared to your old bag of bones." He rushed off.

It was the usual problem. When there was no offspring it was always assumed that the woman was infertile. It was the woman's fault, never that of the man. Yiling and her maid helped the woman stand. Her mouth was bleeding and her clothes torn, for she had been beaten. Thankfully she had normal feet, as she was from peasant stock. Her name was Meeling. Yiling learnt she was only in her early twenties and could see she had been pretty. Her parents were dead and she had no one to turn to. Yiling had to take her back to the Duke's residence, at least for the time being.

Yiling had been eyeing an old, neglected house with many rooms. She had her own funds to purchase it and turn it into a home for abandoned women and girls who would otherwise fall victim to prostitution. There was a Madam in Jian'an who was known to prey on young girls, recruiting them into her House of Little Sparrows. Meanwhile, in the far east wing of the Duke's mansion Yiling placed Meeling, leaving instructions for her to be fed and allowed to sleep undisturbed. In the same wing were also two baby girls found abandoned at the gate one morning.

But Yiling's first duty was to her ailing husband, who seldom went out. He spent his morning hours in the garden, where Bao and Peng would visit, making him laugh with their childish antics.

On the second morning of Meeling's arrival, Yiling found she had brought back a gem. Meeling had discovered the two baby girls and started looking after them, relieving the servants of the job.

There was also laughter from the garden as Bao, Peng and little Lili played together. Then one day there was almost an accident. Peng found Lili at the pebble path leading to Bao's room. She was seated with three piles of stones she had divided into small, medium and large. Peng noticed that Lili had something stuffed in her mouth. Peng tried to persuade her to open up but was unsuccessful. She ran to find Bao and got him to follow her. Bao was able to coax Lili to open her mouth, for the child loved Bao, who always had something edible hidden for her in his sleeve. Out came three pretty pebbles, which looked a little like the cookies from the kitchen. It could have been fatal had she swallowed them. Bao and Peng did not want Yiling worried, so they did not tell her of the incident. From then on they were always checking Lili's mouth. Little Lili simply loved to eat! Her brothers came five days a week for morning lessons. It was a happy group and the Duke enjoyed watching the children at play.

Bao had lessons after lunch as well. In the cool of the late afternoon he would practise sword techniques with the Kung Fu master. Both Yiling and Wu would watch. It made Yiling happy to be reminded of the days when she and her mother watched her father Shan's displays of fine swordsmanship. For the Duke, it reminded him of his younger days, as he had also been a fine swordsman.

Finally, the inevitable happened. Yiling found the Duke's body in bed, cold and almost rigid. It was merciful that he had not suffered much pain. She was sad, for he had loved her and treated her and Bao so well. Bao was only ten years of age. They would both miss him. News of the death was immediately sent to the Duke's eldest son, Hua, in Beijing, and he set off to Jian'an straight away.

Upon his arrival, Hua went through his father's finances. They were in a healthy state. In his opinion, Yiling should inherit the Duke's estate in Jian'an, as there was enough property in Beijing to be divided between him and Wu's other children. Hua and his wife Mi Mi thought the world of Yiling. Mi Mi told her husband that she had not met a person as kind and honest as Yiling and the Duke was most fortunate to have married her! When Mi Mi passed away some years later Yiling made the trip to Beijing to console him.

Yiling thus kept the Duke's mansion, which was her home, plus the home for the girls she rescued from foot binding. She asked to keep half of the guards for security. Of the Duke's antiques she wanted only the jade horse from the Tang period to remember him by. Her own family inheritance was more than sufficient to maintain her charity work.

Yiling's own needs were simple. She was almost vegetarian, except for her love of chicken wings She had little need to spend money and had enough clothes to last the rest of her life. In her study were a few paintings and vases her father's uncle Teck had given her. These were from her father's family and she treasured them. The more valuable family items had been looted or burnt when their house in Jian'an was destroyed.

There was only one thing she needed funds for and that was Bao's education. She wanted the best tutors. Whether Bao wanted to be a scholar or a military person was for him to decide. There had to be enough to help him achieve either. For him she would not compromise! But there was no issue, as Hua left Yiling with more wealth than she needed. Bao was also his father's son and should receive his share. Yiling was reminded that there were honest and fair-minded people in this earthly life.

24

Batir Visits Jian'an

Over the years Batir made many visits to the state of Hu, where Hoong's second group of Flying Horsemen remained stationed at the fortress. Still led by the dedicated Mongol/Han captain, he had not been disappointed for they were well trained, waiting for the day when Hoong would send for them so they could be part of the mighty Ming Army.

There was another reason for Batir's visits to Hu'xinzhou. He had a family there. His partner was a Chinese lady and she had already given him two sons. He took to her his accumulated savings each time. He loved her and wanted the family to live comfortably. She was the aunt of the twins, the two close aides. He also brought back funds from the twins for their Mongol mother. Each return was a happy reunion. Yet Batir was never emotionally tied down. He was a warrior first and foremost, and his place was with Hoong on the battle front.

It had been some ten years since Batir left Jian'an and he felt a strange need to return. He wanted to see the countryside of his youth and perhaps take a peep at Yiling. He knew that Yiling would not recognise him, even if they met face to face. Perhaps it was for Hoong's sake that he wanted to know she was well.

Batir set off for Jian'an and found the Duke's residence near the edge of the city. He saw three children at the front gates. The boy of about ten must be Yiling's son. Curious as to whether he looked like Yiling, he went up to the boy, ready to pretend he was looking for someone in the neighbourhood. The boy looked up at him. Batir gasped and almost fell backwards. His head swam. Had he travelled back in time? In front of him was a young Hoong. The same jaw, the same eyes, even the way he moved his mouth. The only difference was that the child's skin was even fairer than Hoong's. This had to be Hoong's child. He recalled that last evening when Hoong had been out with Yiling. It all fell into place. Bao was looking up at Batir but the stranger appeared to be tongue-tied. Then he muttered something about looking for a Mister Fu and quickly left.

Yiling came out to look for Bao. 'Mama,' said Bao, 'you just missed a strange dark man who was looking for a Mister Fu. He stared at me and suddenly went away. What a queer character!' Yiling thought nothing of it, taking Bao's hand and shepherding the little girls as they went back indoors.

Batir had not gone. He was hidden behind nearby bushes and saw Yiling. She looked well, but of course much older, although still slim. Batir later learnt that the Duke had passed away recently and that Bao was her only child. He learnt, too, that Yiling had taken in many homeless children.

Batir left Jian'an with a secret joy. Hoong was not without family. That trip to Jian'an was worth all the gold in the world. The only question was when to tell Hoong he had a son!

25

Hoong, Special Adviser and Military Commander

When Batir returned to the fortress at the Great Wall he was so excited at the thought of seeing Hoong. The secret he carried from Jian'an would astound him!

But Hoong was not at the fortress. In fact, he was further from his base than ever before. His message for Batir was that he could be away for some weeks and that Batir was to continue training the troops. Batir's special responsibility was the mobile archers. It was imperative that they maintain their speed and agility. There were other capable officers Hoong could trust with the cavalry, for he had often worked with them. The infantry was well trained by the officers as always, besides which, the infantry was not Hoong's responsibility.

As the days passed, doubts arose in Batir's mind about telling Hoong of his discovery at Jian'an. What if Hoong rushed off to see his son? What if Hoong wanted a life with Yiling since she was single again? What sort of life would it be for Hoong and Yiling while they were still relatively young but could not live as a normal couple? What about his work as a military commander? Too many questions and no solutions! Perhaps it was not the right time to tell Hoong what he had learnt. And so Batir kept the secret to be divulged later, at a more appropriate time.

Hoong entered a third year travelling the Wall, fortifying it and working on the best route for the extensions. He took Uxi with him, as they had already done enough for the section of the Wall nearest Beijing. That was the strongest section.

Hoong thrived on hard work. His skin had darkened from his travels and was even more muscular. Each time he returned to base he revelled in the dawn exercises with his Flying Horsemen. Batir felt he had done the right thing to conceal his secret, as Hoong seemed content as the years passed. It was a less complicated life!

Recall to Beijing

Hoong had been working up and down the Wall for nearly nine years when the order arrived to report immediately to Beijing.

Hoong made straight for General Wan's residence, Batir at his side. The following morning, accompanied by Wan and the Minister of War and Defence, Hoong went to the court session at the Imperial Palace. A new threat had appeared in the northwest. Reports reached Beijing that there was a gathering of the Uyghur, Tibetan, Tangut and Khitan tribes. The Tangut tribes from the Xi Xia Empire were thought to be completely destroyed by Genghis Khan and his Mongol army, but it seemed that remnants survived.

The Chinese never forgot Genghis Khan and his fearsome army, or Kublai Khan's conquest and rule of China as the Yuan dynasty. The fear remained that another man like Genghis could arise. The rulers of the Ming dynasty never wanted another foreign power in China. Any rebellion had to crushed, nipped in the bud, if possible. It was the Prime Minister's faction that pushed for a strong army to destroy the enemy near Dunhuang.

But who to lead that army?

Trust the Prime Minister's faction to devise a clever plan – appoint Hoong to lead the army. It would be a dangerous mission. If he died they would no longer have a thorn at their collective side, as he was a staunch supporter of the Minister of War and Defence. If he came back a hero, they would claim credit for having proposed him!

The Minister was trapped into agreement. He appealed to the Emperor to name another leader. Several other commanders had done well in southern China and one of them could be selected instead of Hoong. But the Emperor had other problems, one of which was Princess Min Min. She had never recovered from her obsession with Hoong and was pale and sickly. The Emperor blamed Hoong but was also besotted by his very pretty latest concubine and wanted more time with her. If he agreed to Hoong's new appointment the Prime Minister's faction would leave him in peace. Let Hoong lead an army to Dunhuang.

Hoong was given three months to raise and prepare his army. The Emperor was generous with funding. General Wan and the Minister of War and Defence were ordered to give Hoong assistance. Hoong was promised a thousand elite troops from the Imperial forces, which never eventuated. The Emperor was too canny. His own safety was paramount. He had his brothers to watch and other powerful military figures who eyed his throne! However, the Emperor did send soldiers for the infantry and horses for both the cavalry and Hoong's mounted archers.

General Wan and the Minister's combined influence and power brought about the release of the second group of Flying Horsemen from Hu. Soldiers who had previously worked under Hoong and Batir were also allowed to join the new army. The staging point was at Xian, which was also the eastern starting point of the Silk Road.

Hoong had to be prepared for all contingencies, not knowing what they would be faced with at Dunhuang. They had to travel through unknown and possibly hostile, difficult terrain, through the Gobi Desert and possibly fearful desert storms.

Hoong and Batir were kept busy organising supplies, horses, camels, donkeys to carry the goods and, of course, the men.

Perhaps it was a blessing that the army was not too large, as provisioning was not overly troublesome. Hoong had assembled five hundred men for his infantry, cavalry and cannon masters. Each of the Flying Horsemen teams consisted of fifty men. Then there were the animal handlers and miscellaneous workmen, cooks, doctors and other essential auxiliaries.

The only major problem was that of transporting the cannons, gunpowder and missiles. The wagons were heavy and cumbersome, not to mention dangerous, in hot conditions and rendered useless if made wet. There could be unforeseen obstacles and attacks from tribesmen. The guides would certainly help, but there was always the unpredictable!

The Third Group of Flying Horsemen

In the midst of all these efforts came some pleasant surprises.

One morning, not long after Hoong settled into his ger at Xian, there was a loud commotion. A group of twenty horsemen appeared and were surrounded by Hoong's soldiers. They were Jurchen tribesmen and asked for Hoong. The two young men who led the group were nephews of tribal leader Abu, the man who had agreed to avoid warfare with Hoong some years back. They carried a letter from their uncle.

Abu wrote that his spies had learnt Hoong was leading an army to Dunhuang. His nephews Edmin and Aden, thirsty for adventure, had heard of Hoong and wanted to follow him. The young men were restless and wanted action, while Abu and the older men enjoyed the peace they had negotiated. Abu assured Hoong that his nephews were trustworthy. To them the tribesmen of the northwest were foreigners against whom they would not hesitate to fight.

Batir assessed the tribesmen's fighting abilities, Hoong observing from afar. Yes, they were mobile archers, competent and courageous. They would definitely be an asset to the new army. They came with their own horses and needed little training. Batir added more horse-men to the new recruits, who became the third group of Flying Horsemen. Hoong made it very clear that he would not tolerate any disobedience nor allow any clashes against the other men in his army. The punishment would be immediate expulsion. Batir instructed his nephews to watch the Jurchen group for any suspicious activity.

Lu and Lui turned out to be very useful and hard workers. The twins were devoted to Batir from the beginning, but soon to Hoong as well. The more they learnt about Hoong, the more they grew to love him. They also made friends with Edmin and Aden. Edmin was serious, hardworking and most trustworthy. Aden was spontaneous, fun-loving and mischievous. They were cousins, but Edmin protected the younger Aden like an older brother.

The twins noted another Jurchen youth who often hung around Aden. Mudin was his name, and he had been included in the group because Aden spoke up for him. Mudin hung in the shadows, never saying or doing anything wrong, but he worried the twins. He would never look at anyone directly, seeming to watch from the corners of his eyes. Lu and Lui did not like Mudin. They nicknamed him the scorpion and waited for him to strike.

Mudin shared a secret with Aden: Mudin could imitate the cries of birds. He would do it to amuse Aden, but not when others were around.

Hoong Leads the Ming Army to Dunhuang

It was the day before Hoong and his army left Xian to eradicate the tribal gathering in the northwest. Preparations were complete and there was excitement in the camp. General Wan and the Minister of War and Defence returned to Beijing that afternoon. They had helped to inspect the army to make sure it was fit and ready for what lay ahead. They also deliberated for several days, concerned that the army should be larger. Hoong reassured them it was quality that counted, not quantity. A smaller size meant they could move faster. They also agreed on fewer cannons, and thus less gunpowder. Hoong had been able to convince them that the risk of being stuck in difficult terrain with many heavy wagons was too great.

The General and the Minister were most pleased when they watched a display by the three groups of Flying Horsemen. Batir had worked hard with the new group of Jurchen riders every day since their arrival. The groups moved as if they had been fighting together for years! An extra advantage was their training with swords for close combat.

It was a contented Hoong who asked for an early dinner with Batir, for he did not want to stay up late. Armies always had talented cooks who could produce good meals. This dated from the days when princes and important generals went to war, gourmets who would not be denied reasonable food.

Batir had just gone to his ger next to Hoong's. Hoong was about to change for bed when there was a commotion outside his ger. Hoong's personal guards appeared, bringing in two smallish figures, their faces hidden by hoods. The suspicious pair had been found near the horses and claimed to be horse handlers.

The guards pulled back their hoods and the smaller of the two gasped Hoong's name. Hoong looked. "Wait ... I know this person!" It was the emaciated but still recognisable sweet face of Princess Min Min smiling at him. Hoong invited them to sit.

In a soft voice Min Min spoke. 'My companion is Prince Teng, my cousin, who wishes to join your army and follow you. Please do not reject him. As for myself, I have a wish to make.'

The Princess said she had fallen ill a few months after she and Hoong met all those years ago. The Emperor had the imperial doctors attend to her. They finally diagnosed that she was suffering from an incurable disease and would not last long. Another year had already passed since then, and she did not wish to die in that cold, unhappy palace. Her cousin Teng, her childhood playmate, was the only one who cared for her. Her brother had not seen her for months. The sight of her was too distressing and he was busy with state matters and his favourite concubine. It was Prince Teng who had planned for the last two months and successfully brought her to Xian, to where Hoong was.

Hoong felt sorry for her. He could not send her or Teng back to the Forbidden City. It looked like she had used up the last of her strength in this attempt to see him and would not be able to survive the trip back to Beijing.

He kept Princess Min Min and Prince Teng in his large ger that night. The Princess was so exhausted that she slept right through to early morning. At dawn the army was ready to move. Hoong helped her into a horse-drawn wagon with Teng looking after her. Hoong and Batir had much work to do.

When the army camped before sunset Hoong had Min Min and Teng brought to his ger again. Teng told him the Princess had slept through most of the journey.

Hoong heard her weak cough during the night. Teng was still asleep as Hoong walked to her makeshift bed with a mug of water. Gently lifting her thin shoulders, he raised the mug to her lips. She opened her eyes and smiled at him. She took one sip. Barely audible, she whispered 'I have finished my journey, dear Hoong. Let me rest in your arms.' She looked into his eyes and gave him a smile filled with love. The next moment her eyes glazed over and the hand that gripped his arm fell away. She was gone.

Hoong felt sad for the tragic princess. It was just like Min Min. In life she wanted to help Hoong, not give him problems. In death she gave him no problems either.

Hoong and his army travelled on with Prince Teng and the newly deceased body of Princess Min Min. Hoong and Teng saw a peaceful spot next to the river outside a little town still in Chinese territory, not far from Xian. They looked at each other. Yes, that was where they would bury her. Hoong told Batir to move on with the army. They would catch up.

Hoong and Teng dug the grave, buried the Princess and marked the grave with a headstone they had prepared. The two men rode on to join up with the rest of the army.

Few people knew of Princess Min Min.

The Story of Su

Hoong's army was accompanied by his trusted scouts. His best scout was the young boy, Su, who was recruited when Hoong worked at the Wall.

Su was the son of one of the older soldiers at the Great Wall. He was only thirteen, but had great skill in handling and riding horses. He was small, agile, flexible and intelligent. He brought attention to himself when he jumped onto a runaway horse that was pulling a small carriage with a passenger. The driver had been thrown off. In stopping the carriage and controlling the horse, Su had managed to save the terrified merchant, who had been half asleep, dreaming of his latest profits from selling bales of silk.

The merchant gave him the horse as a reward. On further thought, the tight-fisted merchant threw in a bag of silver. The action arose from his opinion of how much he was worth rather than the boy's courage. Well, that was the end of the matter, thought the merchant as he stroked his bulging stomach and belched.

Su adored his new horse and rode it each day. Half the bag of silver he gave to his mother, the other half paid for the horse's expenses.

Su had two sisters. They were a loving family. His mother idolised her husband but they saw so little of him. She referred to Su as "my husband's son", for his father was never far from her thoughts.

Su loved his mother dearly. He was aware that her joy was great whenever his father was home. He had learnt that his mother was from a well-to-do family with maids. She had been disowned for choosing to marry his father. She suffered much without complaint, even working at a fruit stall so the children had clothes and shoes. She brought up a loving family mostly single-handed.

Suddenly, Su's father started coming home more often, full of praise for the new Assistant Commander Hoong, who, like the legendary commander Yeh Fei, cared for his soldiers. It was a time when soldiers were usually poorly thought of, merely there to serve their country.

Hoong has assessed the situation at that part of the Wall. The Ming dynasty was rich and strong and there was peace. The solders could be given more time off. It would be good for army morale. There had been objections to the increased leave, but these died down when the officers found themselves to be beneficiaries as well. They noticed, however, that Hoong did not take any leave himself.

Each time Su's father came home he would talk glowingly of Hoong. Su learnt that Hoong was a good fighter and a strategist. His father told him of the negotiated peace with the Jurchen tribes, that it was a great victory, for no lives were lost. Had there been war, he could have been killed! And strangely enough, although Hoong was unusually good looking, he was single!

Su's admiration and respect for Hoong grew. Meanwhile, two more male offspring were added to the family. His father's income had increased slightly so they could still manage. This was the family for which Su would gladly sacrifice his life. He would do anything to keep a roof over their heads, warm beds to sleep on and food on the table!

Su was promised by his father that he would be taken to see Hoong one day soon and perhaps be accepted as a recruit. The day came. When Hoong saw a demonstration of Su's riding ability and handling of horses he was happy to accept the boy and Su was with Hoong from that day onwards.

The First Battle En Route to Dunhuang

It was the third morning when scout Su came to see Hoong, for he had a matter to discuss. Before Su began, Hoong smiled and said that he also noticed the dark figures that had been following them from the day before.

Su had details to report. He did not think that the smallish tribal group knew Hoong was leading an army. The cannons had been well concealed and looked part of the goods wagons. Hoong had permitted the senior military men to ride in casual uniforms without armour, as it was warm. Su said they looked like guards. Hopefully, the tribesmen would think that it was an unusually large group of merchants with much protection and would leave them alone.

Unfortunately for the tribesmen, their leaders were not smart. The thought of all the valuable goods they believed were being transported filled them with greed. They licked their lips at the thought of the silks, spices, fine porcelain and so much more. There were horses, donkeys and camels for the taking as well.

Su and the other scouts watched, reporting that they would strike soon. Hoong carefully primed and positioned his army in readiness.

Then they came.

The three squadrons of Flying Horsemen burst forth from behind the wagons, a total surprise to the enemy tribesmen. A detachment of Ming Cavalry was positioned nearby to be used if necessary. Hoong's horsemen had their arrows ready and the first row of tribesmen fell. The second row of tribesmen were too slow for Hoong's horsemen, for they fell too. The enemy turned tail and began to flee, charging into their own men. It was a rout. It was over. Hoong's men were soon picking up the arrow heads and leading away stray horses. That night there were camp fires, rice wine and laughter.

The casualties were low for Hoong's men, while it was many times more for the enemy. Two young tribesmen from the Jurchen group under Edmin and Aden had been killed. They had lacked discipline, rushing out of formation. There were others who suffered injuries.

As his men slept off the skirmish, Hoong stayed awake thinking. He had made the right decision in allowing the three groups of Flying Horsemen to fight without him or Batir leading them. They had been given strict instructions about what to do. Hoong and Batir had stood by watching their progress, ready to ride out should there be a hint of trouble. The Flying Horsemen had done well, passing their first test with flying colours. It had been too easy. The last thing Hoong wanted them to think was that war was easy! It was indeed the opposite.

Hoong gazed across the room and his eyes rested on Tolui's sword hanging next to his armour. A smile came to his lips as he recalled what Batir told him about how the sword had been recovered.

Two years after the sacking of Jian'an, Batir made his first trip back from Hu. He went to a large shop selling expensive items. Batir had a love interest and spotted a tray of attractive ladies' hairpins. After the purchase he glanced sideways and something familiar caught his eye. Dirty and grimy, but still recognisable, was grandfather Tolui's sword. Batir inquired about the price. Surely he could not afford to purchase it, he thought, but could return with the necessary funds. However, it was offered modestly, its real value unknown. Batir quickly said that he wanted it.

The shopkeeper hesitated, thinking to raise the price, as the buyer seemed too eager. Batir quickly turned on his charm, flashed his white teeth and spoke in flawless Chinese. He was better in Chinese than Hoong was in the Mongol tongue. The shopkeeper relaxed and smiled at Batir. He burst into laughter when Batir left, saying 'May you have as many offspring as you have ticks on your body.'

Batir was tempted to keep the sword for himself, but it was made for a taller and better built man. And Grandfather had wanted Hoong to have it.

There was also a story behind the sword. It had been presented to Tolui for saving the life of the heir of a famous military family. The sword had been crafted two generations before by a famous swordsmith. Only three swords of that quality had been made in his lifetime. It was indeed a generous gift from the owners.

Hoong went to bed. There was much to do the next day.

26

The Journey Continues

At dawn Su came to Hoong with the travel plans for the day. They were going to be very busy. Two hours away was a small valley with a stream flowing through it. From there they would be heading into the Gobi Desert. The valley was the ideal place to reorganise and prepare the army for the desert.

They would have to change to travel by camel. The precious horses would only carry minimal loads to make easier their journey through the sometimes sandy, often stony terrain. The soldiers would wear no armour but would still carry their swords. The special supplies for desert travelling were unpacked. Out tumbled rolls of cotton, each long enough to go round the head twice. Every single person was given one. The soldiers were to bless Hoong when they found out how necessary these were. The cotton cloth was to protect their faces from the heat and the sand, flies and other insects found only in the desert. Insects that bite and suck the blood.

From the desert provisions emerged whole batches of different sized containers, again distributed to the soldiers. In them were the miracle creams to soothe insect bites, cuts, bruises, sunburn, cracked lips. Everything one could think of.

The two army doctors claimed their medical supplies. There was a vast array of herbs and balms, including effective pain killers and sleeping mixtures. One of the doctors had worked at the Great Wall with Hoong and a friendship had grown. He had volunteered to join this army and had brought with him his young nephew, also a doctor, but one interested in bones. They shared a hardy assistant who carried his own small mortar and pestle to use on their medicines.

Hoong and Batir had worked hard to prepare for the trip. They remembered the strange turbans of the strangers who visited grandfather Tolui and the stories their uncle Batu told of the deserts and trading routes. They remembered, too, the use of poultices and herbs for cuts and sprains in their large household. And finally, the creams the womenfolk used on their skins for insect bites and protection.

The camels and other animals were well watered at the stream, and the horses had a swim. The soldiers were encouraged to wash themselves, for it might take a week to reach the next oasis. Hoong gave a speech on the dangers of the desert. A new rule was that everyone must go in pairs if they should for some reason leave the camp. Hoong knew that life would become more difficult, so he decided to allow his men to have a relaxed night in the valley.

At dawn the army set off towards the Gobi Desert.

It was not long before they found themselves on the desert sands. Aden was the first to try walking. He slipped off his camel, attempting to stay upright, but planted his face in the sand instead. This brought howls of laughter from Edmin and the younger men, and they learned to appreciate their camels.

The first day of travel was uneventful. The sky was clear, although it was not too hot, but they had not yet gone far into the desert. The surroundings were deceptive. The younger members of the Flying Horsemen thought the desert looked like a beautiful place, not fearsome, maybe warm and that was all. They camped behind a large sand hill and enjoyed a good night's sleep.

The Sandstorm

The army awoke to a haze in all directions. Even the sun was not visible. Neither the faraway mountains nor the close by sand dunes could be seen! The guides and scouts gathered in Hoong's ger. Their advice was to stay put. Venturing out was discouraged, as there were signs of an approaching sandstorm. If the weather changed, if the sun came out, then they could think again.

Hoong and Batir remembered their uncle's voice as he related his adventures. Uncle Batu had wanted to travel into Persia and beyond. He returned to the Silk Road and never came back to Jian'an. News came years later that he had perished in a sandstorm.

They both knew that travelling through the desert never took one route. It all depended on the shifting sands, even in the stony regions of the Gobi. In the desert, the sands dominated, the sands ruled. With the addition of the wind, desert storms were deadly and could destroy whole armies by burying them.

The dunes were sometimes called the "singing sands" for the not unpleasant sound they sometimes made. The "music" ranged from the low murmur of the wind to a shrill siren-like sound, the precursor to a mighty storm. The guides told them the shrill sound was a warning to rush for safety. Large sand dunes built by the wind could function as shelters. In other parts of the desert were "corridors", formed as the wind eroded the sandstone formations into long, narrow walls, also providing shelter for travellers.

While the older soldiers were content to wait out the sandstorm, the younger ones were restless, especially Aden and several Jurchen youths. Aden was now paired with Muni, who followed Aden and did whatever Aden wanted.

Edmin had matured more, but still had great affection for his cousin. He wanted to learn as much as he could about the war and accompanied Hoong and Batir whenever allowed. Aden told Edmin that he wanted a look at the desert and could not wait for the haze to lift. He was tempted to sneak out with Muni, just for a short while, if refused official permission. Edmin spoke with Batir, saying it was only a harmless trip of short duration. And besides, Muni was known to be cautious. Edmin added that Aden had always been a curious child and should settle down after going out. But curiosity was going to kill the cat!

Batir peeked into Hoong's ger, seeing him surrounded by maps and in deep thought. Deciding not to interrupt, Batir met up with Edmin and Aden. He decided that there would be greater safety in numbers. Aden and Muni, another pair of young Jurchens and a pair of young foot soldiers greedy for adventure could take a short trip, the six of them on three camels. Batir added that the group should wait awhile. Hopefully the haze would clear a little.

Batir returned to his ger. There were always matters needing his attention, but he felt uneasy and went again to see Hoong. Hoong's maps were now neatly stacked. Batir quickly told him about the young Jurchens' plans, Hoong immediately responding 'No, too dangerous'. He rushed out with Batir following him, only to learn that the group had already left. They had waited a short while but laughed at Edmin's attempts to delay them further.

Edmin was trying to keep the group in sight as they disappeared into the haze. Hoong and Batir joined him as the visibility suddenly worsened. To send a search party in such poor conditions was unwise. It could mean sacrificing more lives, as there were now more signs of an impending storm. They could only wait and hope.

Then the sands started to sing. The low rumbling sound continued through the night as sand whipped through the camp and all around, stopping just before dawn.

The sun came up as if there had been no storm the day before. As the sky brightened a lone figure and camel was sighted. Hoong, Batir and Edmin rushed out. Edmin prayed to the Earth Mother to please let it be Aden. It was Aden's camel but not Aden. It was his partner, Muni.

Muni said that he did not go far while the others decided to go on. He claimed they would not listen to him and left him with the camel not far from the camp site. Muni had sheltered with the camel behind a dune while the storm raged. The others did not return. When light came Muni was able to find his way back to the camp.

A search party was sent out, discovering one of the camels but no trace of the third beast or the other five souls. Inconsolable, Edmin was moved to Hoong's ger for the night and, on Hoong's instructions, administered a sleeping potion. That ended his weeping but replaced it with snoring that kept Hoong awake half the night. During that night Hoong checked on Batir, who had also been upset for being easy on the youngsters. Batir was dead to the world, also snoring loudly!

The next day the army moved on, quieter than usual, for they felt the loss of the five members from their ranks.

On the army moved into the desert. Unlike other deserts, the Gobi was more bare rock than sand. It was also on an altitude higher than most deserts and the nights were becoming colder. Whenever the scouts reported that all was well, with no enemies in sight, the men were allowed camp fires. The fires and blankets issued to the soldiers kept them warm at night.

The First Oasis

The morale of the army was a priority with Hoong. He expected to be outnumbered by the enemies. He prided himself on the quality of his fighting men, not the quantity. Not one single life should be wasted as far as he was concerned. When the guides reported that they were nearing an oasis Hoong was pleased, not for his own sake, but because the soldiers would have a good break!

The troops were filled with gladness when told they would be arriving at an oasis soon. There were over-stretched necks and red squinting eyes, as each soldier wanted to be the first to spot the desert garden. The Mongol soldiers wondered how they had not realised that Chinese men had such long necks – or had they grown overnight in their attempts to spot the oasis? The soldiers also learnt that there was a good sized town that had much to offer besides Chinese food, especially a hot spring bath where they could soak their weary bodies and feet! There was a stream in which both the men and the horses could swim. Finally, the news that made the troops want to embrace Hoong and Batir was that they would be paid part of their salaries that evening at camp. They laughed at the thought of themselves strutting down the streets with money in their pockets!

Camp was established with unbelievable speed. Then the men were all in line to listen to what Hoong had to say to them. Hoong reminded them that they were civilised troops of the Ming Army, not uncouth wild men. They were expected to behave. No rape, no theft, no bullying. They were not invaders but fellow citizens. Punishment for poor behaviour would be severe. Offenders would be cast out of the army. They would never be allowed to return to Inner China. Then everyone received their part wages.

That first evening everyone felt like they were in a dream. Those who relaxed in the hot water spa would never forget the bliss their bodies and feet experienced. Batir tried to persuade Hoong to join them, but Hoong wanted his men to feel completely relaxed. He left Batir to groan in pleasure with the men as they enjoyed the hot water.

As they emerged from the spa, red as cooked lobsters, the men's shrieks made them sound more like boys as they learnt even more good news. The commander at the oasis had decided he could spare some sheep for a feast. The locals had just had their best season for the livestock. It was the first meal of red meat the visitors ate since leaving Xian. The roasted mutton combined well with the local flat bread. They asked each other 'since when had soldiers lived so well? Word also got around that Hoong and Batir ate what they ate, the same army rations, unlike other commanders and generals. Trust the army grapevine!

After consulting Commander Dee, Hoong decided they would stay at the oasis for three days. The next stage of the journey would be through the worst of the desert, and it was a long way to the next stop. What concerned Hoong was the need for his Flying Horsemen to exercise and practise their manouevres. To the north of the oasis was open land that was ideal. The infantry and cavalry also needed to practise their battle formations. For the three days they all worked hard.

Hoong accepted the invitation to spend the night in Commander Dee's home, as there was so much he needed to know about his new environment. To Hoong's surprise there was a private hot bath in the home and there he inwardly moaned while soaking in the steaming hot water.

It was a relief to find that Dee was a straightforward man. He had a small army and was grateful for Hoong's tips on how to keep his troops fit and well. The Commander had much to tell. They rarely had visitors and no fresh troop reinforcements. Occasionally, a large group of barbarian tribesmen would visit. When they were stronger than his troops he would negotiate. The barbarians would often take livestock and the locally grown grain. The locals would lose some of the womenfolk as well, and often hid their young daughters. They needed a larger army if they wanted to dictate their own terms. They sent regular reports to Beijing as ordered, but received little in return.

Commander Dee communicated with other way stations. Life was monotonous. There were no reports of tribes gathering lately, but this oasis was still far from Dunhuang.

As Dee finished his story Hoong felt something nudging his legs. Hoong lifted the object. It was a small child about two years old. A pair of huge eyes looked into his. Dee laughed. 'Did you escape the maid again, my precious?' The child smiled at her father but made no attempt to leave Hoong's arms.

'Ah, it must be the fur on your boots. It reminded her of the little rabbit she had.'

Hoong pictured the time when Yiling squealed as a rabbit ran over her feet. This child was like the daughter Hoong imagined he could have had with Yiling had their lives been normal.

The bold toddler stretched her chubby fingers towards the little dessert cakes on the table. Her mouth was small and crumbs remained on her lips as smacking sounds emerged. Still she remained in Hoong's arms. Before she was handed over to her father, Hoong learned that her mother was a local girl. Always sickly, the mother had passed away a few months earlier. Dee, coincidentally, was from Jian'an. He had drifted to this outpost years ago, but of late was thinking of going back to Jian'an, for he still had family there. He would take the child home.

The three days came to an end. The soldiers readied themselves to continue the journey but there was one final unpleasant task Hoong had to perform before leaving the oasis.

Five soldiers were brought before the assembled troops. They had broken Hoong's rules. Two of the infantrymen were charged with attempted rape, another with drunkenness and assault. Two young men from the cavalry had been caught beating up a restaurant owner and his waiters for poor service and lack of respect. They fell on their knees, begging Hoong for a second chance. Hoong reminded them of his speech on arrival at the oasis. There was no place for them in the army anymore! They were transferred to the control of Commander Dee. If they proved themselves good workers and reliable they had a chance to become citizens of the oasis or to join the army there.

Some of the soldiers thought Hoong harsh, but the majority thought him to be fair. They also now had a better understanding of army discipline and of Hoong's standards.

27

Hoong's Army

Three days at the oasis gave Hoong time to check on his special recruits. These were the men who had a particular attachment to him. On the second afternoon he made time to see Prince Teng, cousin of Princess Min Min. The Prince had done exceedingly well in the army, impressing Hoong with his courage and intelligence, as he had shown in his escape with the Princess from the Palace. He started off as a horse handler because of his love for the animals, but was to discover he also had people skills, for he had a kindly disposition. Teng did not have a mean bone in his body.

As the son of a minor concubine of one of the Emperor's brothers, Teng had been the target of much spite and bullying. Within the toxic atmosphere of the Palace he was a very unhappy child. His cheerier moments were when he played with Princess Min Min. No one abused him then! Plus, Min Min would feed him the sweet cakes he loved. She was the person he loved most in his life.

Prince Teng found his place in Hoong's army when the head of the cavalry asked if he would like to join them. He was an expert horseman. He also found that he was well able to handle the required weapons, the swords and the lances. His comrades appreciated him and were proud to have a prince in their ranks!

Hoong found Teng had fitted in and was content with his new life. Teng told Hoong he had finally found life worth living and was much happier than he had ever been in the Palace. The well-being of his men meant much to Hoong. With a light step he proceeded to look for Edmin, the Jurchen youth.

Hoong saw Edmin from afar many times, but he wanted to have a leisurely chat and a cup of tea with him. Of late, Edmin was more cheerful and alert, finally recovering from the loss of his cousin Aden. Edmin informed Hoong that his Jurchen warriors were doing well and had no complaints. He thanked Hoong for the enjoyable break at the oasis. Muni, Aden's good friend, worked quietly with the others and always behaved. Hoong had never taken to him because of his shifty eyes, but now decided that he was only a harmless young fellow. There was no need to watch him. Unfortunately, this was one of Hoong's few mistakes in judgement and it almost cost him his life.

Hoong never neglected his Flying Horsemen. On the last morning at the oasis he exercised with the first and second groups of Flying Horsemen, spending time with them afterwards. They would always be special. The first group often made him laugh. Hoong was young and relaxed when he first trained with them all those years ago. He had often tried out new manoeuvres with them, and they had seen him fall off his horse when he over-twisted his body.

And Hoong never forgot the Wu brothers, Li and Tu, for when combined it was "Wu Li, Wu Tu" which meant muddled or confused in Mandarin. They were from southern China, where their names were perfectly normal. Then there was handsome Wen, whose mother was Mongol, and joker Lin, who would often do his cross-eyed act to the amusement of his companions.

The second Flying Horsemen group was a rougher and more cheeky group. One member was Moe, who had a fine voice and loved to sing. He was often bursting into song. Another member was Po of a hundred moles. He stood out for his face was covered with the dark spots. He also had a shrill voice and was referred to as everybody's girlfriend.

The third group of Flying Horsemen was perhaps not as close to Hoong, although they showed him deep respect. While the other two groups had a long history with Hoong and Batir, this third group was partly made up of the Jurchen tribesmen who had followed Edmin to join up with Hoong with the blessings of Abu, the Jurchen leader.

As for the Ming cavalry, it was made up of the horsemen who had worked with Hoong at the Great Wall. Hoong was also a cavalry commander and had often practised with the men there, although he chose to ride with and lead the mobile archers. They were delighted when the Minister of War and Defence obtained their release to join Hoong's army. The Minister had also obtained another detachment from further south to join the cavalry under Hoong.

The infantry was less familiar with Hoong. They came from the armies of others under the Emperor's orders.

Hoong learnt that emperors expected much but gave little. It made Hoong wonder what it was that made soldiers so faithful. What made them willing to die for a man they had never seen? A man who did not hesitate to throw away thousands of lives in battle!

Then there were the individuals who served Hoong faithfully and interacted with him often.

Su, the scout who reported regularly. Su checked each day for hostile groups in the neighbourhood. Hoong had arranged for a large sum of money to be handed to Su's father for the dangerous work his son did. Su was also training another three men as scouts.

The twins, Lu and Lui, who looked upon Hoong as family. They were like the soldiers who were willing to sacrifice themselves for their emperor. The twins worked hard. The hours they spent on the horses and archery were rewarded by their admission to the first group of Flying Horsemen.

A team that worked silently, avoiding attention, was the gunners. They were a small group of large men with incredibly strong arms who worked with cannons and gunpowder. They were in charge of the few carts carrying these weapons, pulled by oxen. These beasts had been included as they could be used for food when the gunpowder was used up. Again, it was quality that Hoong had. Both men and weapons were the best that the Ming dynasty had to offer. And the gunpowder had vastly improved since the earlier years. The gunners came from the most sophisticated section of the Great Wall. These men knew Hoong well from the years he had worked with them.

But it was not the cannons on which Hoong depended. It was his Flying Horsemen, whom Hoong considered had the skills for battle in northern China. Hoong had brought spare horses along. Both he and Batir kept a special eye on the horses, which were maintained in as good condition as possible throughout the journey.

It was Hoong's army. Few commanders would know their army as well as Hoong did. He was loath to lose a single man, whether through battle or illness. Every life mattered!

And of course Hoong had Batir, who was always there.

One could say that Hoong devoted himself whole-heartedly to his army, for that was all he had!

28

Onwards to Dunhuang

It was a cheerful army that left the oasis, only to be replaced by tired faces and red eyes as they journeyed on. It was sand, sun, insect bites and monotony for the next three days. Their speed, already moderated by the conditions, was dictated by the slowest part of the army, the wagons carrying the cannons and gunpowder. They were not burdened with too many wagons, nor by rain or mud, so they had a relatively easy time. However, on the third day from the oasis they had to shelter from a sandstorm. Again, they were lucky, as it was only a minor one! By this time their stay at the oasis seemed a lifetime ago!

On the next day they came to a small settlement that only survived because of a nearby river. Its small population claimed to be Chinese. Their leaders guided Hoong's army to their partially hidden valley. The army had some hours of pleasure splashing in the waters, while Hoong and Batir were pleased to see the horses washed and refreshed. There was even some fresh pasture for them.

Hoong learnt that there had recently been a raid by a marauding tribe. The livestock and other food had been taken, as well as the young women. The remainder had to beg for their lives. The older folk asked Hoong to take them and their young children, as they did not want to be subjected to further attacks. Hoong explained he had a mission to fulfill and there was no way they could care for the old and young. He left some of his precious food supplies for the pitiful lot. And so the army moved on.

Another four days of travelling in the Gobi Desert, relentless sun by day and freezing temperatures at night.

Su was constantly with the guides, working on the route. They made a decision to veer north. After half a day they came out to grassland as if by magic. There were whoops of joy from the soldiers, as they were on solid ground again. The scouts checked that there were no tribes about and the army made camp. The horses and other animals were allowed to graze on the summer grasses. The soldiers needed to practise their battle formations.

That night Hoong ordered extra rations for the troops, a much needed reward and morale booster. They still had some way to go to reach Dunhuang, although the guides reassured them they were not far away.

The following day the army moved southwards again, back into sandy terrain. Another two days through the desert. On the third day the scouts reported there were small groups of tribesmen around, each numbering less than ten members. The next day there were more of them. They were surveillance groups, keeping their distance. It was clear that they were not there to fight, but to watch. Hoong's orders were to continue on, to retaliate only if attacked.

Then they sighted the fortress of Dunhuang. They had arrived.

29

Dunhuang

Dunhuang was a fortified settlement located near a small oasis surrounded by high mountains on one side and the Gobi Desert. The Dang river flowed down from the mountains, supplying much-needed water. Merchants and travellers from Persia, Greece and India met in Dunhuang, the trading centre and the most western outpost in China. While many Chinese merchants went no further, the Mongol tribes under Genghis Khan's sons moved beyond, engaging Russians and Islamic states in battle and defeating them.

The paintings, the sculptures and engravings at the Mogao caves nearby revealed much about the distant places to the west. Roman warriors, Grecian ladies, Indian paintings of the Buddhist gods, as well as portraits of the wealthy, high-class Tang dynasty ladies who donated to the development of the caves were found there.

Semi-autonomous at times, Dunhuang's past had been turbulent, variously falling under the control of the Han and Tang dynasties, and at one stage was the centre of the mighty Xi Xia dynasty. The Xi Xia were utterly defeated by Genghis Khan, after which the entire region came under his grandson, Kublai Khan, and the Yuan dynasty. The Chinese maintained a garrison there during the early Ming dynasty, as the Uyghurs and Tibetans had been active in recent times.

The commander of the Dunhuang garrison greeted Hoong and Batir with great joy. An army had finally arrived from Beijing! Hoong and Batir immediately went to work placing cannons in the best spots around the fortress walls. Then deciding on where the stationary archers should be located. Their main concern was an early attack, for Hoong needed time to plan and organise. At the same time, the troops were setting up their camp inside the fortress walls.

That night Su tracked down Hoong, for he had urgent business as well. There was something he wanted Hoong to see.

Batir was needed at the camp, so Hoong took Lu and Liu with him. Su led them to the base of the nearby hills. They tethered the horses to some fir trees and, together, crept up through thick foliage. Su had done his job well, for spread out below them, a little distance from each other, were three camps, with small campfires dotted through-out. Flags helped identify two of the three groups. The grandest camp belonged to the Tibetans, much simpler was that of the Uyghurs. The largest group of the three was a collection of small gers of different colours, sizes and quality, clearly belonging to a mixture of tribes. It was too dangerous to stay watching and Su signalled that they should leave.

Thanks to Su, Hoong had been able to see that his enemy was in fact a collection of distinct groups. It was not a unified army. Hoong could tell that hostility and mistrust between the tribes still existed. The inherent weakness of the tribes was there!

On their return, Hoong instructed Flying Horsemen groups two and three to rest, leaving group one on watch. The rest of the army had also been given permission to sleep, as everyone was exhausted from travelling. Su assured Hoong that there was very little likelihood of an attack that night.

Batir joined Hoong for a short discussion. The two warriors agreed that the longer the tribesmen took to attack the better for them. Sun Tze's teachings were most reassuring. While Hoong's army was outnumbered, they were disciplined warriors, well-drilled, trained in battle formations and skilled with weapons. They fought as one army, fiercely loyal to Hoong and had great morale. These were the army's strengths. Its weaknesses lay in the hostile environment and the unknown adversaries. And, of course, the larger number of fighting men they faced. Hoong and Batir slept well, for they had learnt something of their enemy!

Early the next morning, Hoong inspected an old section of the Great Wall near the fortress. Here were stretches of a rammed earth wall, the tail of the Chinese dragon that began on the east coast at Shanhai Guan, the Old Dragon Head. Fascinating, but probably not much use in battle, he thought.

Hoong was fortunate to get the precious time he wanted. Time for the army to settle in. The gunners busily cleaned the cannons and dried the gunpowder. The stationary archers checked their weapons and familiarised themselves with their positions on the fortress walls. The infantry wanted to know where they would sleep when they were not fighting. The horses were exercised.

Since setting out from Xian, the men did their exercises daily. Even after a long day of riding Hoong had his troops exercise before dinner. A remarkable group was the gunners, who practised their kung fu movements every time they stopped, even during the half hour before meals. Seeing is believing. How could such heavily muscled men move so gracefully? If the enemy was expecting an army of flabby, unfit fighters they were in for a surprise!

Hunan

The scout Su's contribution was valuable, allowing Hoong his first look at the enemy. Su also told him that the most aggressive and active group was the collection of various tribes that roamed around under a mysterious leader.

The powers in the area were the Tibetans and Uyghurs, who each looked upon the other tribes with disdain. Of late they had become alarmed. News reached them that a new leader of the Tunguts, called Hunan, was drawing together the "lost tribes" that roamed the area north of Dunhuang, numbering several hundred men.

Hunan had an interesting background. His father was a Chinese commander sent to Jiayuguan with a Ming army in 1372 to help with the construction of the Great Wall . He had fallen in love with a tribal princess and Hunan was the result. Unfortunately, the commander chose to return to Beijing, abandoning the mother and child.

Hunan did not inherit the best physical attributes from his parents. His Han eyes were the smallest in the tribe. He had his mother's flat nose and small build. Hunan grew up hating the Chinese, for his mother told him his father had no qualms about leaving them.

But Hunan was not without talent. An intelligent and natural leader, his horsemanship was equal to the best in the tribe. Perhaps he inherited his father's abilities with weapons and military skill. He used the sword and the lance expertly. Those around him noticed his talents. Others respected and feared him, as he had little hesitation in killing. He would have attacked Hoong's army on their first night at Dunhuang but for the fact that the Tibetans and Uyghurs wanted to wait and study their enemy. It annoyed him to lose that advantage but he needed them to cover his back. He knew that the Ming army led by Hoong would be too strong for his tribes alone.

Hunan's strategy was different. He dressed like his fellow tribesmen, not wanting to be identified. He would only come forward with his wild battle cry at the most crucial part of the battle. It had worked in all his battles. Hoong, in contrast, led from the front. His soldiers looked to him and took courage from the impressive, imposing, larger than life figure that they loved.

Hunan made elaborate plans. His network of spies was able to get artists to sketch a good likeness of Hoong's face. Copies were made and distributed to the tribesmen. Hunan's order was to isolate and kill him at any opportunity. That would be his key to victory. Meanwhile Hoong and his men had no idea what Hunan looked like.

War Games: A Peek into the Past

The four year old ran as fast as his sturdy little legs could carry him from the west wing to Tolui's study and up his sleeping body. When his lips reached Tolui's right ear, he whispered "Little Hoong can whistle as good as Ba. I can show you."

Tolui was treated to a clear small whistle. The doting grandfather could only smile at his precious grandson.

Hoong and Batir played their whistling game daily. It was their special call to each other. The uninitiated would assume it was an unusually loud bird. As the boys grew they perfected their whistling, working on it so the sounds came out loud and clear. These calls were to become the battle signals for the Flying Horsemen: when to attack as one unit, when to split, and when to surround the enemy. Groups one and two started to practise this at Hu'xinzhou, group one continuing during the years at the Great Wall and group two when Batir made his regular trips back to the state of Hu.

Since Hoong and Batir wanted the whistling signals kept secret and only for combat, the mobile archers often practised without the battle signals. On the occasions when the calls were used, the horsemen were instructed to listen and remember to the best of their ability. Hoong and Batir managed to emit extremely high-pitched whistles to distinguish themselves from other whistlers. They often followed up with different bird calls.

The first group of Flying Horsemen were the most familiar with the system, as they had trained the longest under Hoong and Batir. The second group was a most enthusiastic group, although they had trained more with Batir than Hoong. The third group had trained the least, as they had joined only in Xian. Hoong and Batir had a special meeting with them to explain the battle formations. They had also gone through the whistling signals, which could be given by either Hoong or Batir.

The cousins were happy with the Jurchen group under Edmin and Aden. They did not doubt the sincerity or loyalty of the young Jurchen leaders. They were all excellent horsemen and mobile archers. Hoong could not ask for more. On the long journey to Dunhuang the only time the whistling signals and the formations were practised together was at the area north of the oasis. When there were no roaming tribes around.

Except there was someone who listened and watched. He was also an expert at bird calls. Muni, from the Jurchen tribes. The only one who knew his secret and had been fascinated by his imitations of bird calls was Aden. But Aden was dead and dead men tell no tales!

30

Hoong's Poems from Dunhuang

It was only on the second night that Hoong was able to slip out of the fortress to study the mighty dunes a short distance away. His sensitivity and the tragedy of his castration seemed to have deepened his awareness of the beauty around him.

Hoong rode his horse carefully past the snoring soldiers, who were still exhausted from their journey. Hoong had been lucky with his horses. This was the second horse that moved with him as one. Grandfather Tolui told him that this would happen. His first beloved horse had been smaller in size, more like the Mongol ponies, but he had lost it in battle. But like the first horse, this one also seemed to read his mind via small movements on the reins. Even when Hoong's hands were on his bow and arrow and he gripped the horse with his legs it knew where Hoong wanted them to go!

Approaching the towering dunes, he felt the silence and beauty of the desert. A half-moon enhanced the ethereal, somewhat eerie scene. Turning around to retrace his steps, it seemed to Hoong that the fortress was suspended in mid-air.

Ode to the Sand Dunes

You look magnificent,
Standing tall in the moonlight.
Formidable, with a look of permanence.
The beauty of the sweeping slopes,
And the gentle peaks,
A scene of perfection.
Yet these are but sand hills,
Vulnerable to the mighty desert winds.
Winds that can flatten them and sweep them away
Alongside the puny men who traverse them.
So feast your eyes on the beauty of the desert scene
Enjoy it while you can.
In a day it may be gone.
Impermanence too has a place
In this world of ours …

The Desert Rose

One cannot stop the strong wind from blowing
It is buffeting the bud among the little pile of rocks
Yet it cannot force the bud to open.
The howling storm threatens,
But the desert rose survives.
Out comes the sun,
The unrelenting heat cannot force the petals to open!
Night comes, the air turns cool.
A movement ever so tiny.
Slowly, slowly the petals open out.
A rare crimson beauty is there for all to see,
But who in the desert can witness that!
For a few short hours its beauty stands defiant,
Then the petals fall,
It is no more.

So too, our lives on this earth,
For within our human souls lies great beauty.
Steadfastness, resilience, strength, compassion, sacrifice, love …

Time
In this vast world of ours,
Know that our lives are not of our choosing.
When we com-eth
When we go-eth.
We lament its shortness.
In truth, one lifetime is enough for achievements.
For creativity has no limitations, no boundaries.
Look back through the centuries,
Let us look at the good
While we are aware of the evil.
The many lifetimes that have shown
If we are willing, we can.

31

The Battle of Dunhuang

A dark mass was sighted on the horizon at dawn on the third morning after Hoong's army arrived at Dunhuang. As it moved towards the fortress at Dunhuang, and as the sky brightened, the darkness resolved into the figures of armoured men on horseback holding swords. They accelerated as they neared the fortress. The front rows parted and out came mobile archers with their bows and arrows. The enemy forces rode on, expecting to take the defenders by surprise.

Out through the fortress gates galloped the three groups of Flying Horsemen, bows at the ready. Hoong was leading them. Hunan's men were stunned at the speed at which they came. The first ranks of the enemy tribesmen fell to the arrows of the Flying Horsemen. A second lot of arrows flew fast and true and more of the enemy tribesmen fell.

Then came two sharp whistles followed by a bird's warble, which was the signal for the Flying Horsemen to split. Out shot a figure in a black cloak, waving at the Flying Horsemen to follow him away from the enemy! Batir usually wore a black cloak but it was not Batir. He often led with Hoong, but once in a while would ride behind the other horsemen. That morning some instinct told him to stay at the back. The moment Batir heard the two whistles he knew something was wrong. They were not from Hoong! The whistles were just a pitch too low and the bird warble was different. To the second and third group of Flying Horsemen it sounded very similar and they started to veer away, even though there was no reason to split.

Batir immediately urged his horse forwards towards Hoong. He threw his hood backwards to show his face and stood up on his horse. He gave the signal for the horsemen to return and fight as one force, but precious time had been lost!

Hoong was isolated. Only some twenty of his Flying Horsemen were with him, but they formed a circle around Hoong to protect him. There had been much shouting from the enemy tribesmen, for they had recognised Hoong from the sketches Hunan had distributed.

Hunan now emerged from the middle of his formation with a shout to his troops. He had sized up the situation. There had been either a blunder or treachery. Here was a godsend opportunity. And the Ming cavalry was engaged with the Uyghurs, too far away to save Hoong!

Hunan stopped his forces from attacking Hoong. He wanted to enjoy the kill himself. Hunan was going to behead this renowned, revered, military hero with the outstanding good looks all by himself. Hunan would be famous after he held Hoong's head before all on the battlefield.

Hoong shouted to those around him to save themselves, but his beloved Flying Horsemen preferred to die with him. From the first group were twins, so too Edmin, the brothers Wu Li and Wu Tu and Handsome Wen. From group two were Po of the hundred moles and Moe the singer. They had spotted Hoong and chose to ride behind him.

Hunan, by slowing down the action to kill Hoong himself made a vital mistake. Batir had ridden like the wind. He had regathered the rest of the Flying Horsemen and come thundering to rescue Hoong. They charged at Hunan's forces and the two armies were suddenly fighting again. Batir hacked his way through to Hoong. When Hunan realised what was happening he gave orders to kill Hoong's circle of defenders. But true to the military expert's skill and speed, Hoong lunged at Hunan, forcing his grandfather Tolui's sword through his chest.

It was Batir who decapitated Hunan and, bellowing a warning to the enemy, held the grisly head aloft. Already failing against Hoong's better trained men, Hunan's tribesmen quickly lost the will to fight. They turned and fled.

Meanwhile, the Uyghurs were steadily losing to the Ming cavalry and infantry and became confused when they saw Hunan's tribesmen fleeing from the battlefield. The commander of the Tibetan soldiers, who had yet to engage, felt his better trained troops should be kept for another day. He ordered them to turn for home.

As the shadows grew long, Hoong's wounded soldiers were taken back into the fortress. The dead were buried. Stray horses were gathered, reusable arrowheads and weapons were recovered. Hoong's Ming army had prevailed, but there was no great rejoicing, for in war only death is the winner.

32

Aftermath of the Battle of Dunhuang

The week following the battle was a sombre time. The death toll, while not heavy in number, included important members of Hoong's army. Younger twin Lui had thrown himself in front of Hoong and been slashed to death. Elder twin Lu was inconsolable. His hands on his forehead, Lu repeated over and over "I love sharing my face with you, Lui. I am so miserable and lonely without you. Why did you leave me?"

Brothers Wu Li and Wu Ti and Handsome Wen had been killed. Po of a hundred moles and singer Moe also died while protecting Hoong. There were others dead, including half a dozen of the Jurchen tribesmen. The wounded included Hoong with a shoulder injury, Batir with leg injuries and Edmin, who lost three fingers on one hand. Still others with wounds and broken bones kept the two physicians busy.

Edmin insisted that the treacherous one from his tribe be brought to justice. The person who had imitated Batir, the figure in the dark cloak who had given the whistling signal to the horsemen to split and ride away, had been caught. Muni from the Jurchen tribes had tried to sabotage the battle and get Commander Hoong killed. He had almost succeeded. Why?

Muni was brought, bound in chains, before a committee of seniors that included the three wounded leaders, Hoong, Batir and Edmin.

He defiantly admitted being an expert in whistling and bird calls. He had imitated the vital call. From his kneeling position he turned to Edmin, asking whether he remembered the two Jurchen brothers, both captains, who opposed Abu's decision to negotiate for peace at the Great Wall. Those brothers had tried to start a rebellion. They had been caught and executed. The elder brother was Muni's father, the younger brother his uncle.

To Muni it was all Hoong's fault. He hated Hoong from that time and vowed revenge.

While the senior men debated an appropriate punishment, Edmin knew what he had to do. One of his tribesmen had almost destroyed a Ming army. As long as he lived, Edmin would live in shame. Drawing his sword with his uninjured hand, Edmin plunged it into Muni. Most of the troops felt it was the right decision.

Another serious matter had to be decided. There were some eighty prisoners from Hunan's tribes, many wounded. The more aggressive Ming officers wanted them executed so they would not be a problem in future, nor would they have to feed them. But Hoong disagreed. He interviewed them all and decided that the very young ones could be trained into loyal soldiers, animal handlers, or do other useful jobs at the fortress. The few older ones were released to rejoin their families.

Message from Beijing

Six days after the battle, an imperial decree arrived from Beijing. Speedy communication to and from Beijing was possible, for Hoong had rejuvenated the relay stations along the route to Dunhuang. At the height of the former Mongol power there had been relay stations all the way along the Silk Road, from Xian to the middle eastern and Russian lands. They were known as yam stations and were serviced by yam riders. In those days the stations had spare horses and hot food for the riders. Messages could be passed to fresh riders and horses and carried over vast distances. No other powers could compete with the Mongols in sending news. On their way through, Hoong had made repairs, left horses, capable men and funds to have the relay stations working efficiently again.

The decree conferred on Hoong the title of General to reward him for his success at the battle of Dunhuang.

There was also a personal letter to Hoong from the Emperor. While he congratulated Hoong, the Emperor did not consider that the work was finished. Hoong was given new instructions, which were to destroy the Tibetan power so there were no longer tribes to challenge Ming rule. He left it to Hoong to use his expertise to achieve the goal, since he was so strong and capable. Thus there would be no reinforcement of troops from Beijing!

33

Life Continues in Jian'an

Life in the residence of the late Duke Wu continued to be lively. In the far west wing lived ten female children between the ages of five and ten, looked after by a staff of five women. These children had been in danger of having their feet bound, so were brought home by Yiling.

Sadly, there were unscrupulous people who preyed on others. Women who bought female children from the poor, fed them, and sold them to brothels when they were old enough. The pretty ones commanded a good price, while the plain ones were candidates for foot binding. Some families would purchase female children as brides for their sons or as concubines for the old master of the family. Others had different motives, such as the childless women who wanted a servant to look after them in their old age in their own homes.

Yiling was realistic enough to know she did not have the unlimited funds such charity work demanded. She did what she could.

There was also her other charity, one for abandoned or widowed wives, women who were abused and discarded. She had purchased a sizeable property for them years ago. At least these women could look after themselves. They tended the large vegetable garden in the grounds, growing enough to feed themselves and sell the surplus in the market. There was a flower and herb garden, products they could also sell in the market. The cost of maintaining the place was low, as the women did minor repairs and painting. At regular intervals, Seng

179

would take the male staff from the Duke's residence to do whatever difficult work the women could not manage.

In the main residence were three growing children. Peng was now a teenager. She had impressed on Yiling that she had no interest in marriage and begged to be allowed to stay. She proved herself capable in so many ways. She had learnt much from her father and kept the flowering plants in excellent condition. There were always displays of the flowers in season in the main sitting room.

Peng took over running the kitchen, including the provisioning, when the old chef retired. She had an assistant, a talented woman who did the cooking and supervised the kitchen staff. There were no longer elaborate meals with the Duke gone. Yiling ate simply. Only Bao needed his meat dishes. He was not a fussy eater, although he appreciated good cooking. Yiling, Bao, Peng and Lili enjoyed their healthy and tasty meals each day.

What Peng did best was look after Lili. From a chubby toddler, Lili had grown into a beautiful healthy child. Throughout the years Lili loved to follow Bao and Peng. She would stretch out her plump arms for Bao to carry her. It was Bao who stopped her tantrums and crying, turning them to giggles and laughter!

It was a largely satisfying life for Yiling. Bao was growing up with decent values and started to help Yiling with the running of her two charities. He checked that the funds were properly spent, that the staff were capable and doing their work well. Yiling noticed that although Bao had Hoong's looks and build, he had a more studious nature.

Yiling ensured that Bao could handle weapons, had good swords skills and no stranger to horses. However, Bao was more interested in books than in the military. He told his mother that he wanted to sit for the imperial examinations. He wanted to join the bureaucracy and serve the country in that way.

It was always at sunset on the fifteenth day of the lunar month that Yiling's thoughts turn to her past. She would sit in the garden and think of Hoong and her parents. Bao noticed and left Yiling to her thoughts. He particularly discerned the sadness in her eyes and her face on those days.

As the moon rose, Yiling's thoughts drifted to the bamboo forest, to the young boy and girl, the peace and contentment they had found with each other. Was he still alive? If he was, did he ever think of the bamboo forest and of her?

34

Hoong Prepares for War with the Tibetan Tribes

At Dunhuang, newly appointed General Hoong had a big problem to solve. He had been ordered to destroy the Tibetan tribes but not given the means. The Emperor was not sending reinforcements, neither troops nor weapons. The Tibetan tribes were fresh, as they had not taken part in the battle of Dunhuang. Hoong's Flying Horsemen largely destroyed Hunan's tribes, but at the cost of a number of casualties. How was he going to find replacements? The Uyghurs were badly defeated by the Ming cavalry and infantry, but there were men lost from that encounter. The cannons from the fortress had found their targets, but the limited supplies they brought had been halved. Did the Tibetans have cannons to blow up the walls of the Dunhuang fortress? Probably so, but surely inferior to the Ming army hardware and gunpowder. Hoong's wounded soldiers needed time to recover. Even he and Batir had to recover from their wounds. Elder twin Lu was in deep depression from the loss of his brother. Jurchen tribal leader Edmin was still in shock from Muni's act of treachery.

It was a troubled Hoong who sat in his ger when Su asked to see him. Scout Su had been busy. He had just returned from Jiayuguan, a fortress town Hoong did not visit in his haste to reach Dunhuang. Su reminded Hoong that there were Ming soldiers in Jiayuguan, sent to protect the builders and provide assistance with the construction of the Wall. So there were the much needed extra soldiers. They would have with them weapons and ammunition, possibly cannons. Hoong was buoyed by the new information. He had been too preoccupied to think of Jiayuguan.

Strange that the Emperor had not given orders to visit that fortress. The emperors of the Chinese dynasties had always been a suspicious lot, continually looking over their shoulders, fearing mutiny and death plots. Did he worry that Hoong would conspire with others, such as the forces at Jiayuguan, to overthrow him?

Su was still with Hoong when a messenger rushed in. A few tribes had appeared, requesting to join Hoong's army. Was it more good news? Hoong agreed to meet their leaders. Two men entered Hoong's ger. They asked that a specific ex-prisoner from Hunan's men be allowed to join them. The tribesman Arul was found and brought in. Hoong had recognised him as a frank and honest person and accepted him as a new trainee for the Flying Horsemen. Arul had been in Hunan's army because his uncle had made him join. He had not enlisted voluntarily.

The two young men told Hoong they wanted to be soldiers and serve him. Arul vouched for them. They and their men had stayed away because they did not want to fight for Hunan, for whom they had no love. Hunan had killed their relatives. They had no love for the Tibetans, who were arrogant and treated them like dirt. They could relate to Hoong, as his ancestors were also tribesmen. They had also learnt of Hoong's compassion and unwillingness to kill except when necessary. And they knew of other wandering tribes who wanted to join Hoong. If Hoong was willing they would bring them in.

Suddenly Hoong had new recruits for his Flying Horsemen, Ming soldiers from Jiayuguan, plus cannons and gunpowder superior to that of the Tibetans. He could hardly believe the new developments. Although still outnumbered, he had an army that could put up a good fight and win!

Hoong was almost fully recovered, while Batir could ride better than he could walk. Together with Su, they rode at dawn to Jiayuguan and met the commander of the fortress. Hoong outranked him. Hoong pointed out they were both officers serving the same country, the same emperor. If Hoong's army fell to the Tibetans it would not augur well for the fortress at Jiayuguan. The commander agreed.

Su suggested that the new recruits from the wandering tribes should train at Jiayuguan, away from the eyes of the wily Tibetans, as their scouts and spies had already targeted Dunhuang. Jiayuguan was a half day's travel away. Batir could station himself there and supervise their training. While the Tibetans were familiar with Hoong's face and figure, Batir was not so well known.

Su and his team were out each day, trying to learn as much about the Tibetans as they could. When would the Tibetans strike? Both groups played a waiting game.

And so the months passed.

Meanwhile, the Tibetans had their own problems. The commander who watched the battle of Dunhuang and withdrawn his troops had advised a quick attack on the fortress while Hoong's army was still recovering. Unfortunately, the prince who supported him had fallen out of favour and a rival prince had the ear of the old ruler. They were overly cautious and wanted to watch and wait. The waiting favoured Hoong. His new recruits grew strong, the army at Jiayuguan blended in well with Hoong's troops, and the wounded recovered. Hoong's gunners received extra cannons and gunpowder and prepared themselves for the enemy attack. Those training at Jiayuguan were ready to travel Dunhuang at a moment's notice. But when would the Tibetans attack?

The precious months were what Hoong needed, but a long game was not what he wanted. The Tibetans were in their own territory and comfortable. Hoong and his army wanted to finish their job and return home. They could not wait indefinitely.

Again, it was Su who went to Hoong with a plan. He felt that the Tibetans had been distracted by their internal politics. They were not aware of what was happening at Jiayuguan, so had no idea of how well the training under Batir was proceeding there. Su's plan was to get the Tibetans to attack the Dunhuang fortress.

Su offered to allow himself to be caught by the Tibetans. He would carry the plans of their holiest temples and pretend that Hoong's army was about to attack and burnt them all. That would hit a nerve. The Tibetans would certainly not allow their holy places to be destroyed!

Hoong knew the plan would work, but was unwilling to sacrifice Su. Su reasoned with him. He was under no illusion that his work was dangerous and that he was dicing with death at all times. Su had no wife or children. His parents and siblings had been provided for. Su knew that Hoong had left his father with a large sum of money and that his family had enough for a good life. Besides, if Hoong lived, he knew that Hoong would make sure that they were well cared for into the future. His sacrifice was double, for his family and for his country. He would endure torture and he would die happy.

Hoong said no to Su's proposal but knew he was determined. Hoong extracted a promise from Su. He must stay alive and return to the fortress.

Hoong was solemn when he emerged from his ger and walked along the fortress wall in the bright moonlight. It was the fifteenth night of the lunar month. He cast his eyes onto the barren ground of the Gobi to the east of the fortress. In the west was the Taklamakan desert, to the south was the Tibetan Kingdom, only a short distance away. In the distance, behind the fortress to the north, lay the Altai mountains. As he stared at the scene around him, another picture came into his mind. Sadness clouded his face. It was a beautiful vision of a bamboo forest. On a large fallen log sat two figures, a young boy and a girl. Hoong shook his head, he could not afford the luxury of lingering on the scene. A battle would take place the next day. He might not survive. Life was unpredictable, he knew only too well. But he also knew that he would never return to the desert. He walked back to his ger amid the snores of his men.

At dawn Hoong woke to a busy day before him. As Su and his scouts rode out of the fortress gates, Hoong prepared his army and the fortress for the forthcoming battle. It was to be the last battle. They had to destroy the Tibetan power, there was no second chance!

Su and his team rode until they could see the large buildings that were the temples of the Tibetans. His scouts were instructed to stay back and watch. Su had faith in his plans and expected, as a result of being "caught", that the Tibetans would quickly mobilise their troops for a massive attack at Dunhuang fortress. At first sign of this activity, his scouts were to ride like the wind back to Hoong to tell him that the Tibetans were coming.

Su rode obliquely towards the temples, careful not to be caught too early, for he was an experienced scout. It was a while before he knew he was followed and a while more until he was surrounded by a group of Tibetans that included spies and soldiers. He was punched and kicked before being bound and taken to one of the commanders. When he was stripped and found to be carrying plans of the temples he was sent to the Tibetan army leader.

Su was indeed tortured, his fingernails ripped off one by one. He was in intense pain before "confessing" that Hoong's plan was to burn all the Tibetan temples. The war committee was summoned. As the temples were involved, the religious patriarchs joined the committee. These old men held much power.

While they met, news reached the committee that a fierce fire was consuming one of the most important temples. The senior elder monks were most alarmed and agitated. They thought the fire must be the work of Hoong and wanted revenge. In truth, the fire at the temple was an accident. As the second oldest temple it was managed by a number of old men. One of them had stumbled while replacing the large red burnt out candles with fresh ones and fallen. His robes had caught fire. The fire had spread. Everything was old and flammable, and it was a roaring conflagration by the time the alarm was raised. The streets were narrow and the rescue effort difficult, resulting in the deaths of some of the elderly carers and a burnt out temple.

What happened was heaven sent for Hoong. The religious elders could not be placated and they swayed the elderly ruler. Even though the Tibetan troops were not prepared for immediate battle they were sent out to war. His scouts raced back with the news of the Tibetans' movements.

Amidst all the chaos, Su's best and most devoted scout managed to sneak into the Tibetan complex and find Su. He was able to load Su onto a horse and, with unbelievable luck, they swiftly made their way back to the Dunhuang fortress. In earthly life such luck does happen.

Hoong was watching at the fortress tower, his troops ready and waiting. He saw the scouts and had the gates opened as they drew near. Su fell into Hoong's arms, murmuring 'I kept my promise', and lost consciousness. The two physicians immediately set to work on Su with their acupuncture needles.

Hoong's horse was readied to lead his troops against the Tibetans, who were now racing towards them.

35

The Last Battle

General Hoong's army was in readiness, awaiting the attack of the Tibetans. Hoong had chosen his time and place.

The Tibetans were not quite ready. Their decision to strike was not made by the military but by religious old men with no concept of war strategy or timing. They knew they outnumbered the enemy, and that gave them confidence. Their religious convictions made them feel that their gods would help them to punish the ignorant men who tried to harm their temples.

There was much haste and confusion as the Tibetans ran to join their battalions. The gunners could not move their equipment quickly and were left behind, even though they were needed to smash the fortress walls before hand-to-hand combat could begin. This meant that the cavalry and the Tibetan horsemen would have to lead the attack instead. The horsemen who were mostly without armour, as they had time only to grab their swords, bows and arrows and some shields.

Hoong's gunners fired as soon as the enemy came within striking range, causing death and confusion. The Tibetan front ranks fell to the scattered cannon shots. Many of the Tibetan horsemen following lost their shields. The stationary archers at the fortress drew their bows and the arrowheads flew into the unarmoured horsemen. What a pitiful sacrifice of Tibetan fighters!

More Tibetan warriors surged forwards, but Dunhuang's gunners continued to mow them down. Finally the Tibetan cannons arrived, to the cheers of their soldiers. There was a halt to the firing from the fortress. Then the Tibetan cannons came into action.

Hoong's gunners watched, ready to fire again. The largest of them shrieked with laughter as the enemy's cannons misfired and blew up their own men. The Tibetan cannons had not received the loving care that the Ming gave theirs. The cannons had jammed, the gunpowder was not dry enough and the gunpowder mix was inferior to that of the Ming army! More misfires and more laughter from the gunners before some of the shots hit and damaged the fortress walls. But by then the Ming gunners had destroyed most of the working Tibetan cannons.

It was time for the rest of Hoong's army to engage. The Flying Horsemen followed Batir, Hoong led the cavalry, and the infantry ran behind. After the action of the cannons and stationary archers, many a Tibetan horseman was left holding only his sword. The Flying Horsemen had their bows ready and arrows rained down on the enemy. The Tibetans combatants could not believe the speed or dexterity of the Flying Horsemen, let alone their courage, as they did not seem to fear death. They were stunned by the changing battle formations of the Flying Horsemen as they fought. Those who had heard of Genghis Khan and his warriors now understood how they would have fought. The Tibetan mobile warriors were no match! Hoong's Flying Horsemen under Batir slaughtered many.

Hoong led the Ming cavalry straight into the Tibetan ranks. In the use of the long sword, lance and close battle short sword, the Ming soldier was yet again second to none!

As the battle raged on, the advantage of Tibetans numbers no longer held true. Of the still-living Tibetan soldiers, many turned to flee rather than be dead at the end of the day! Quite a few of the officers were religious and patriotic men who felt ashamed of those who chose to flee or surrender. They fell on their own men and killed them.

As evening fell there were not many left alive on the Tibetan side. The wandering tribesmen had done much killing, too, for their beliefs taught them not to show mercy if they wanted to be successful.

Hoong and Batir were victorious. Again, Hoong did not rejoice in the deaths, but he accepted that was part of his life as a military man. When negotiations were not possible he had to kill to survive. Those were the basics truths of war – and his orders from the Emperor.

The next few weeks were busy. There were the bodies of the dead to deal with. Burial for Hoong's men and, at the request of the Tibetan leaders, cremation for the enemy. Hoong allowed the few wounded Tibetans to return home, a concession he made because so many of their soldiers had been killed. It would be a long time before they could build up their power again. And perhaps longer for the memory of the defeat to fade!

Hoong and Batir had to make plans for Dunhuang and Jiayuguan, even as they nursed their own wounds. They had to leave behind able administrators and troops to maintain Ming power. Some of the men wanted to go home. Su was one of them. He had been saved by the physicians, but was still weak. His injuries were serious and needed care. Prince Teng had distinguished himself in the Ming cavalry and wanted to return to Beijing. Lu, the surviving twin, wanted to go back to Jian'an. There were Flying Horsemen from Jian'an and Hu who wanted to return. Others in the army had family elsewhere they wanted to see.

Conversely, there were those who never thought of leaving. These included the wandering tribesmen who had joined Hoong's army. For the soldiers from Jiayuguan, Outer China was, or had become, home. Inner China was foreign. They would continue to serve the army in Jiayuguan. Besides, some of them had married tribal women from the surrounding area.

Luckily for Hoong, Edmin decided to stay at Dunhuang, and the surviving Jurchens from the third group of the Flying Horsemen chose to stay with him. Edmin told Hoong that his uncle Abu would have died by now. He did not want to rejoin the old tribe, as Aden's relatives would be a constant reminder of his dead cousin. He did not see any future in working outside the Great Wall in north-eastern China, but believed he would have a meaningful life at Dunhuang. In addition, Hoong must have noticed that the wandering tribesmen looked to him as next in command after Hoong and Batir. With Hoong and Batir gone he would be their sole leader. With their army, the Flying Horsemen would be the strongest in the region now that the Tibetans had been utterly crushed.

Edmin assured Hoong that as long as he lived he would uphold Ming power. He was indebted to Hoong and loved and respected him, so Hoong could trust him.

With matters settled in Dunhuang and Jiayuguan, Hoong could start preparing the return to Inner China. Meanwhile he continued to train the troops at both towns. It was during this time that Hoong started to visit the Mogao Caves nearby.

The Mogao Caves

Within riding distance to the south-east of Dunhuang were the Mogao Caves, also known as the Caves of a Thousand Buddhas. Hoong had wanted to see them but only had the time after defeating the Tibetans. There were reportedly some five hundred temples dug into a cliff face, a treasure trove of Buddhist art. Buddhist monks were reputed to have started painting the walls a thousand years ago. The monks isolated themselves in the caves, meditating for weeks, months, even years. The resulting artwork was some of the most beautiful Buddhist wall paintings, engravings and sculptures. As the Caves became known pilgrims came by the dozens, including Chinese Buddhist monk and scholar, Xuanzang.

It was said that Xuanzang visited the Mogao Caves in 629 AD. He is credited with translating the sacred scriptures of Buddhism from Sanskrit into Chinese. He had been a pilgrim in India for sixteen years and was the inspiration for the Chinese classic *Journey to the West*.

Hoong was able to make several visits to the Mogao Caves, now abandoned by the Buddhist faithful as the northern trade routes were slowly supplanted by sea trade and the desert sands encroached.

As he wandered through a few of the caves, marvelling at the richly decorated surfaces, Hoong knew who would really appreciate it. That person was Yiling. On his first, last and only night with Yiling they had seen a Tang dynasty court scene painted in the caves near the bamboo forest back at Jian'an. Hoong saw similar images here. The Tang influence on Dunhuang was great. Rich benefactors had sent workmen to the Caves to paint portraits of themselves and make carvings of Buddha, expecting to receive blessings in return.

On his third visit, Hoong stood near the back of a cave, facing the entrance. A seated Buddha, his attendants and other deities posed gracefully behind him, glinting in the rays of desert sunlight that managed to find their way in. As Hoong admired the mural to his left he noticed an unusual shadow on the design. Intrigued, he started scraping with his dagger through the ancient, dried mud, making a hole just large enough to see into a small hidden room. Inside, Hoong could make out piles of innumerable manuscripts.

Carefully enlarging the hole so he could reach inside, Hoong pulled out several of the manuscripts. On one he made out the name of Xuanzang. Could these be the holy sutras Xuanzang had brought back from India? Hoong decided he would take back to Beijing a small part of what he found as a gift to the Emperor. The rest he would leave to be discovered by future generations.

Hoong carefully resealed the wall, dampening the fragments of mud with liquid from his leather water bottle.

Hoong's last visit was quick. He checked his handiwork on the cave wall. The damage he had done to the mural was barely visible and he did not think the secret room would easily be rediscovered. Hoong took a last look as he left the cave and said goodbye. He would never come this way again.

Goodbye to Dunhuang and the Desert

It took many weeks of preparation before Hoong and the residual of his army could leave.

Finally, Hoong had done everything he could for Edmin and the fortress at Dunhuang. Edmin and Arul stood in front of the Flying Horsemen group made up of the remaining Jurchens and wandering tribesmen. They would maintain Ming power in Dunhuang. The men saluted the departing army. Edmin gave the famous whistle of the Flying Horsemen, the whistle for the troops to advance. Batir had taught him the various whistles, although Edmin could never produce it like Hoong and Batir did. Then it was cheers and a last hurrah. Edmin had to turn away, for he was in tears. They would never meet again. Hoong and Batir showed great control, but Su, Lu, Prince Teng and many of those who came with the original army cried unashamedly. They would never forget Dunhuang, nor their dead comrades, no matter how keen they were to return home. Then they headed towards Jiayuguan, where they would stay the night.

At Jiayuguan they were welcomed by the Ming soldiers who faced the Tibetans with them. A bond had been created. Were all men brothers after all? Out in the desert, in hostile country, men who hardly knew each other had fought with and for each other. Affection and trust had grown between them in the short space of time. They rushed to hug each other when Hoong's army arrived.

True too, strange men had tried to kill them. They had been told that they were enemies who threatened and would kill them given the chance. They had responded likewise! Were men not strange? Hatred and Love? It was all so complicated!

They feasted that night, drank and fell asleep next to each other, some with arms and legs on each other. They were sad to part the next day. A few of the badly injured soldiers with no family in the east chose to stay upon learning that the younger physician was remaining in Jiayuguan. So all was well.

But Hoong still had half his original army. These were men who had no families, no one for whom to leave the army, and they had found friendship there. Even so, many had misty eyes as they embraced their new-found friends for a final goodbye. They thought, too, of those taken by death, those who had fallen in battle or from illness on the long journey.

It would be a long trip retracing their steps, but this time there were no wagons carrying cannons to slow them down. Su's scouts came with them, as did their original guides. There were ever-present dangers crossing the Gobi Desert. But there were no known large hostile tribes, and even if there were, they would be foolish to take on Hoong's army. There were spare horses and camels, plus fodder for the animals. There were supplies for the men, rice, wheat flour and dried meat. And enough livestock to last at least to the large oasis near the beginning of the desert. The return journey would definitely be much faster.

Some days before they left Dunhuang, Batir had spent an entire morning talking with Hoong. They greeted each other with smiles, as there was time for camaraderie now the battles were over. The time had come for Batir to reveal his secret.

Hoong knew Batir only too well, seeing he had good news to tell. He recognised the glint in Batir's eyes and the happiness on his face. They had clasped each other's arms, not needing words to express what was in their hearts. Together they had survived the journey and the battles. Both were glad to be returning home. Then Batir blurted out what he had kept in his heart for so long, fearing to hurt the little cousin he had loved since his birth.

"Hoong, Yiling is alive!" From Batir lips came the story of the old Duke. That Yiling had married a man old enough to be her father. He had been her saviour. Yiling had thought that Hoong had been killed. The Duke had since died and Yiling had brought up a male child thought to be the Duke's son. He, Batir, had visited Jian'an and seen the ten year old boy and Yiling. All this before the long journey to Dunhuang. The boy was not the Duke's son, for he was the image of Hoong. As sure as the sun rises he could only be Hoong's son. Even the way he moved his mouth was like Hoong!

Hoong was speechless. He had bottled up his emotions for so long! Tears came to his eyes and he wept. It was the first time Batir had seen him cry as an adult. Hoong gripped his hand in silence. Batir could see Hoong grappling with his deep feelings for Yiling. Then a slow smile spread across Hoong's face, a rare joy that Batir was privileged to see. That it was Hoong who experienced it gave joy to Batir. In a soft, wondering voice Hoong exclaimed 'I have loved ones to return to. I have a son!' Batir left Hoong to ponder what he had just learnt.

Outside Hoong's ger Batir left instructions for Hoong to remain undisturbed. Any urgent matters were to be brought to him.

36

Homeward Bound

Hoong's army had matured, having been through so much and away such a long time. Time and experience had made them stoic, more accepting of life and its challenges. They were a cheerful lot. A bond had developed between the men and there was an attitude of care and concern for each other in the camp. The older physician was returning to Inner China with the army and he checked on Su and the other wounded patients.

For the next two days the weather was slightly hazy. Travelling was a little easier without the scorching sun. On the third day the sun came out, but the sky was still not clear. The guides felt that these were signs of an impending storm. On the fourth day they came to a small oasis.

Hoong, Batir, and Prince Teng had a discussion with the guides and scouts and decided to camp at the oasis for two days. It was a wise decision, as the desert storm did materialise. Although only a medium storm it could still have given some problems. Then it was back on the camels again as they headed towards Xian.

Two days of relentless sunshine, no talking, lips dry and cracked. Hoong had released the last of his supplies at the start of the return trip. The soldiers were thankful for the fresh white cotton coverings for their heads and faces and the ointments for their hands and feet, but there was none of the lip balm left. On they went. Then the large oasis where they had rested for three days on their forward journey came into sight. Despite their cracked lips, the whoops of joy still came from the soldiers.

Commander Dee came out to greet them. Hoong had walked but a dozen steps when he felt a tiny pair of hands round his left shin. He looked down to see two dark eyes staring up at him. Hoong smiled at her. 'You remembered me, little Jin Jin?' She tightened her grip as she grinned back. How could I forget you, her eyes said! Hoong swung her above his head as laughter broke out across the group.

Hoong and his army was welcomed back and there was feasting that night. This time it was not just mutton but an assortment of meats. The speciality of the night was roast pork, a big hit with the foot soldiers. Since they were last there a big farm of pigs and chickens had been established. By whom? That evening, after a good hot bath and short rest at the commander's home, Dee escorted Hoong to the feast. Two grinning men came forward to meet them. Hoong felt they were people he should know but he could not place them, as the older man was plumpish and the younger man had filled out too. They look at Hoong with affection.

One was the drunken foot soldier, the other the officer who had assaulted a small restaurant owner. They had been expelled from Hoong's army for breaking his rules. The foot soldier came from a farming family and had experience with pig farming, while the officer from the infantry had brains. They had become good citizens, worked hard and prospered. They learnt from Hoong. They knew that without his disciplinary action they would not have made anything of their lives. Of the other two foot soldiers, one had died from a drunken brawl, the other worked as a swordsmith. As for the other cavalry officer, he was a merchant and away, otherwise he would also be at the feast. As they finished talking a huge man stepped up to Hoong and bowed deeply. He was the swordsmith, the former infantry soldier. He burst into tears, begging for forgiveness. Hoong patted his arm telling him everything was past and over with. The man's shoulders heaved with relief as the weight of self-loathing was lifted from them. Together with the other two, he went to look for Batir.

Hoong went to bed with peace of mind, knowing that the soldiers he had punished and left behind had done well.

The next morning was spent with Commander Dee. He told Hoong he had waited for him to return. The time was now right for him to retire. He had been training a younger man to succeed him and would return to Jian'an. Going with him were his deceased wife's two nephews, orphans whom he had brought up. They were as brothers to his daughter, having grown up together. Dee had no doubt they would fit in with his siblings' families in Jian'an. Hoong was happy to have them join him.

Hoong was starting to enjoy family life. Jin Jin looked on him as a second father and her teenage cousins likewise. Batir had admitted to having a Chinese wife and two sons in Hu'xinzhou, which Hoong could see made Batir feel fulfilled. Yet life was full of hellos and good-byes, joy and sorrow.

With light hearts Hoong, Batir, Prince Teng and Commander Dee left the oasis with their men and the children. It would not take long to leave the sparse Gobi Desert of Outer China behind them. Another two days and they were in fertile, populated Inner China once more.

Hoong and Batir decided not to return to Beijing, and wanted to find a quiet spot where they could spend two nights to say a final goodbye to the army. The soldiers had been their family for so many years! They had given enough of themselves to their country. While other commanders and generals had their breaks and time with their families, Hoong, in particular, had served continuously. Both Hoong and Batir had worked tirelessly at the Great Wall and then in the desert. Their bodies could take no more. The rest of their lives were to be spent leisurely with their loved ones. Those in the army were also to be given the chance to live lives of their own choosing. Hoong would tell them there was no compulsion to report back to Beijing. No one would be the wiser as to whether they had died in battle or gone missing in the desert. And indeed there were some who suffered battle fatigue or had no wish to see death and bloodshed again.

Commander Dee told the guides of a beautiful little city not far from Xian.

That first night at the quiet city, Hoong and Prince Teng conversed into the night. Prince Teng could not thank Hoong enough for his new life. The army career suited him. He had risen to the challenges. He was still young but already in the senior ranks. Hoong met with the military seniors and Prince Teng was selected to lead the army into Beijing since Hoong would not be returning. Teng promised that he would never raise Hoong's name except to the Emperor and only to let the Emperor know how great a leader, fighter and strategist he was. Let the politicians in Beijing speculate that Hoong had died in battle, that it was too painful a subject for members of his army to talk about!

That night Hoong wrote a personal letter to the Emperor.

Hoong emphasised that his body was tired and he no longer wished to fight. He was worn out. He had never taken leave, never had time for leisurely pursuits, no time for himself at all. He had served his Emperor and country at the two most difficult locations, the Great Wall and in the desert. He apologised for his inability to do more. He suggested that his absence from Beijing could be beneficial, as there would possibly be less tension at Court for those who feared or were envious of him. He finally thanked the Emperor for having honoured and trusted him.

Together with the letter was the parcel of manuscripts from the Mogao Caves to be handed personally to the Emperor. There was a deep bow from Prince Teng and a farewell embrace. Another sad goodbye.

The next night Hoong spent drinking with his officers and soldiers. He seldom imbibed and, as usual, knew his limits. The next morning a small group of some fifty split from the army. Hoong and

Batir led the small group towards Xian, while the army rode on to Beijing.

At Xian, Su's elderly parents, siblings and their children greeted them. Hoong watched Su's joy. It was another sad goodbye. More goodbyes with the others who were leaving the army to lead their own lives. Perhaps after a year or so, a few would return to travel into the desert as merchants and meet up with their old mates at Jiayuguan and Dunhuang. Who knew?

Batir's sons, now young men, were there to meet their father and uncle Lu. Hoong, Dee and the children stayed that evening in Xian.

Early the next morning they set out for Hu. Hoong witnessed the happy reunion of Batir and his wife. It gave him pleasure, for Batir meant so much to him.

Dee intended to stay at Hu for several days, as he had things to do.

The next day Batir's sons escorted Hoong to the outskirts of Jian'an and, at his request, left him. It was only a short distance to where Yiling lived. He wanted to be alone when he met her. Hopefully he would see his family as well.

37

The Reunion

Yiling's simple house was situated just outside Jian'an. There were no displays of luxury, but it was comfortable. Its beauty lay in the gentle breeze that came with the setting sun, even more so from the moonlit nights with the mountains in the background. It was a good place for reflection, meditation, solitude. A good-sized property with rooms for when son Bao, wife Peng and their two children made their regular visits from Beijing, as was currently the case. Bao, like Yiling, loved nature and tranquillity.

Yiling was up early. She tended to her pots of white orchids, which were in full bloom. She could not help the smile that came to her face, although it was somewhat sad and wry. In her mind she travelled into the past.

Was she ten years old when Hoong, with his mischievous smile, was obviously hiding something behind him? It was during one of their meetings in the bamboo forest. With an exaggerated movement of his arms he had brought forth a beautiful spray of white orchids. It was from grandmother Yanni's garden. Grandfather Tolui personally tended to the garden. Yanni had died early and Hoong had never met her, however, Tolui had told him so much about her. It was Hoong's favourite flower and had become Yiling's favourite as well.

Yiling cast her eyes on the rough road that led to the property. She saw a figure in the distance but thought it must be a farmer or hunter. She was not worried. Bao had insisted on two guards stationed at the outhouse at the back of the property. Their presence was unintrusive but they were trained to be available at a moment's notice!

She went on tending to her plants but kept glancing at the road. The figure continued to approach. Perhaps it was somebody looking for Bao, for he was an important Ming official. Something told Yiling to keep looking. The figure entered through the gate and approached her. She sensed it was someone she knew. Her instincts were seldom wrong. The person was familiar, someone from her past. His hair was still dark, but shot with silver streaks. He was tall, his shoulders wide, but he moved with a slight limp.

The thought of Hoong sprang to her mind but it was not possible! She had grieved deeply when news reached her that he must have died fighting near Dunhuang. The victorious Ming army had returned, led by a young commander. There had been no sign of Hoong.

She had last seen him when he led his army through Jian'an on his way to Beijing so many years ago. That beautiful image of him, the high nose, the stern face. He looked magnificent in his armour. Tears came to her eyes as she looked away.

Then the voice, 'Yiling, Yiling'. No, it is not possible! She must be dreaming. A hand stretched across to touch her. 'It is me, it is Hoong!' Her eyes opened wide like a startled wild animal and a strangled sound escaped from her lips.

It was Hoong! His face was lined but still handsome and smiling. He had changed yet he had not! She could never mistake the image she had locked in her memories. She flung out her arms to embrace him. Yes, it was Hoong's laughter. Her joy was so great she felt that this was the moment she had lived for. And the moment she could die for!

They were in each other's arms. Hoong's strong fingers wiped the tears that flowed uncontrollably down Yiling's cheeks. The noise from outside brought Bao out to check on his mother.

The two men eyed each other. Neither could believe what they saw! Hoong saw the image of himself in the younger man. Bao saw the older man he would become, the same eyes, nose, square jaw and even the build! He knew he was looking at his father. Even as a child he believed that Duke Wu was not his father, despite the care and love he received.

Bao had never questioned his mother. He knew of the attack on Jian'an nearly nine months before his birth. He had thought of the possibility that his real father was a soldier who had raped her. Now he understood the sadness she carried. His biological father was the man she loved.

Yiling felt faint and sat down. For Hoong and Bao there was no need for words. They embraced each other. Bao's son refused to be left out and clung on to his father's arm. There was a slight tug at Hoong's leggings. He looked down to see a three year old girl with Yiling's eyes looking up at him. Hoong's heart over flowed with love and joy. He had family. A son, a grandson and granddaughter.

Peng came out and saw her husband's father for the first time. She was intelligent enough to understand the significance of the scene. She went back to the kitchen to prepare food for the happiest day in the lives of her loved ones.

Yiling insisted that Hoong share her large room and bed. She was not going to allow him to be elsewhere. Their love was that of the older generation, no longer of fiery youth, but a gentle enduring love. Perhaps the true meaning of love. A love of tenderness, just to touch each other, to enjoy each other's presence. Yiling wanted to touch Hoong's face, to brush back his soft greying hair with her fingers, to lean against him. This was enough. This was joy, this was total bliss.

Just before dawn, Yiling woke from a deep sleep. What a wonderful dream she'd had. But then, her eyes still closed, she felt something move, and became aware of the sound of gentle breathing. She forced her eyes open. It truly was Hoong with a head full of hair and a still muscular body. It was no dream. She wept with joy. Hoong opened his eyes and smiled at her. Yiling responded with that beautiful smile. It was the smile he carried with him all those years. The smile that was before him when he lay for a hundred days after castration, when he was denied water except to moisten his lips and the little that went into his food, when he thought he must surely die. It was the same smile that flashed before him when encircled by the tribes at the battle of Dunhuang. When he expected Hunan's sword to pierce his body.

Could Hoong believe that he was now in this beautiful place with Yiling and his family? Here he sat with Yiling in his arms watching the sun set. The next night they had witnessed a wondrous full moon against the mountains. Yiling fell to her knees to thank the moon goddess for her blessings.

Batir appeared a few days later, aided by his sons, his legs still weak from battle injuries. It was from Batir that Bao and Yiling learnt of Hoong's hard life. Batir also described the herbal medicines Hoong needed to reduce the pain from the numerous injuries he suffered fighting for his country.

Hoong and Yiling were formally married that week while Batir was with them.

Peng was able to purchase wedding attire for both bride and groom in the city. The clothing was traditionally red in colour, without elaborate sequins and beads, yet dignified, for both the material and cut were of the best.

Yiling wore her treasured jade hairpin under the fine red veil. The exquisite hairpin was a gift from Hoong at their last meeting in the bamboo forest. Grandfather Tolui had shown Hoong the jewellery box of grandmother Yanni. He told Hoong that the jewellery in there was for Hoong to give to his wife on their wedding day.

Somehow that day when Hoong went to meet Yiling, he'd had a strange feeling that he should present that exquisite jade item to her. He had gently placed it in her hair. She was wearing it the day that the soldier nearly attacked her. It was on her when she was rescued and taken to Duke Wu's residence. It had never left her possession, for it was a reminder of the happiest days in her life with Hoong. The Duke had assumed it was her mother's.

Hoong was a striking figure in his wedding attire. His height, wide shoulders and muscular body made that inevitable. Plus his strong face with good features. A graceful, slim Yiling stood beside him. They were both no longer young, yet few couples could come near them in looks. Happiness radiated from them. The wedding day was a gift from the gods. They could not ask for more! Again, that wedding night brought them great joy, for they were married at last and never had to part again.

38

The Ending

Hoong and Yiling had five years together. Five years of happiness. It was more than they had asked for or expected. They spent each sunset and moonlit night together. Every moonless night of myriad stars was just as beautiful, needing just the warmth of the other. Over those years many visited them. Each little reunion gave pleasure. Each parting left a question, would they meet again?

Batir visited often with his family, including Lu. Su came, brought by his younger brothers, and Prince Teng came dressed as a civilian. Teng brought a letter from the Emperor agreeing to Hoong's request, and would not summon him or Batir to battle again. Commander Dee came often with his family. There were others who would have come had they known where he was and that he was alive.

Every opportunity was spent with Bao's family. Grandson Wen carried the family likeness. Peng gave birth to a third child, another girl, whom they called Li. This child looked even more like Yiling than the older girl. Hoong and Yiling were surrounded by love.

The years of ceaseless work, his war injuries, not to mention the unseen effects of his castration, caused Hoong's early death. He went at the end of the fifth year after his return to Jian'an. He went quickly, still with his good looks and thick hair, leaving a stoic Yiling, who knew she would follow soon.

Bao found her dead several days later. She looked serene and at peace. Bao had both his parents buried quietly, as was their wish.

News came a few months later that Batir had succumbed to his war injuries. Bao hurried to Hu for the funeral.

A year later Bao had a memorial service for both his parents. Those who wished to attend were welcomed, but it was still a private service for those who were very close.

Bao had prepared Yiling's residence for the service. The visitors started arriving at noon. An old man and a slightly younger one greeted Bao, explaining that they had worked with Hoong and Batir at the Great Wall. It was the scholar Wei, whom Hoong had rescued. The other man was Uxi, the talented engineer and builder Hoong had discovered at the Wall.

Next there was much commotion, for Prince Teng arrived with his private guards. Then came Batir's sons and the surviving members of the Flying Horsemen, who had never lost touch with Hoong. They were from the first squadron plus a couple from the second, led by Lu, the surviving twin, who was also Batir's nephew. Commander Dee was there with Jin Jin and his nephews.

They were all shown to the small ancestral hall that Bao had built and paid their respects to the Laing Family. It was the Chinese family name selected by Tolui. There were the family tablets to Tolui, Yanni, Yu and Yin, Hoong and Yiling, and the latest, Batir.

Then the ceremony started. The famous whistle call of the Flying Horsemen sounded. It was made by Batir's elder son, taught to him by his father. It was so like Batir's call that shivers ran up the spines of all who heard it.

Then something mysterious ... a light swept through the room in the form of Hoong with his arm around Yiling, each with an ethereal smile for everyone in the hall. The vision was gone as suddenly as it came. But the crowd knew what they saw!

On Yiling's tombstone was inscribed: "Yiling, beloved wife of General Hoong, mother of Bao and grandmother of Wen, Lin and Li." On Hoong's tombstone was: "Hoong, glorious Ming General, husband of Yiling, father of Bao, grandfather of Wen, Lin and Li."

Yes, General Hoong, no more the eunuch warrior!

39

Photos from Dunhuang

On the right-hand wall of Cave 16 is the window-like entrance to Cave 17, known also as the Library Cave, at the Mogao Caves. In the early 11th century the entrance to the Library Cave was sealed with mud and the entire wall painted over with a mural. Photo taken by Aurel Stein in 1907.

The author and editor at the Mogao Caves, outside Dunhuang,
June 2025

Crescent Oasis in the Gobi Desert, outside Dunhuang, June 2025

The Gobi Desert, Dunhuang, in the early evening, June 2025

Bactrian camels in the Gobi Desert, Dunhuang, June 2025

The author and editor camping in the Gobi Desert, Dunhuang, June 2025

www.ingramcontent.com/pod-product-compliance
Lightning Source LLC
Chambersburg PA
CBHW071151180726
48291CB00007B/2412